WHERE THE BODIES ARE BURIED

A. S. FRENCH

NEONOIR BOOKS

ALSO BY A. S. FRENCH

Crime Fiction and Thrillers

The Astrid Snow series

Book one: Don't Fear the Reaper

Book two: The Killing Moon

Book three: Lost in America

Book four: Gone to Texas

The Ophelia Red series

Book one: Ophelia Red

The Detective Jen Flowers series

Book one: The Hashtag Killer

Book two: Serial Killer

Book three: Night Killer

Book four: The Killer Inside Them

Northern Crime Fiction

Where The Bodies Are Buried

Crime Short Stories

Call Me: An Astrid Snow Short Story

Dark Snow: An Astrid Snow Short Story

Bette Davis Eyes: Detective Flowers Short Story

Writing as Andrew. S. French

Science Fiction

The Time Traveller's Murder

The Mercy Sleep

Bodies

The Arcane Supernatural Thriller Series

Book one: The Arcane

Book two: The Arcane Identity

Book three: The Arcane Quest

Book four: The Arcane Ultimatum

The Ella Finn Fantasy Novella Series

Ella and the Elementals

Ella and the Multiverse

Ella and the Monsters

Ella and the Dreamers

Supernatural Short Stories

Dead Souls

The Shadow

Go to www.andrewsfrench.com for more information.

1 HOME

A pig's head was waiting for us on the doorstep. It sat in a pool of purple liquid glistening in the wind. My father pressed his walking stick into the eye, making a popping sound like a burst balloon. When he removed the wood, what looked like gristle came with it. He waved it in the air, and the stink of rotten meat punched me in the nose.

It didn't seem to bother him as he stepped over the head and placed his key in the door. Someone who had landed at Normandy beach at eighteen and witnessed the liberation of Auschwitz less than twelve months later wouldn't be fazed by this. And I'd seen a whole lot worse in my forty-five years.

As he entered the house, he glanced at me through a face that hadn't, to my knowledge, smiled in my lifetime. His ninety-three-year-old bones rattled in the doorway, his mouth open to show me those yellowing teeth.

'Halloween's come early this year.'

Only it wasn't Halloween, it wasn't blood, and the pig's head was plastic. The messages to me from the locals had increased in frequency and design, from obscenities scrawled on toilet paper shoved through the letterbox to this latest exaggerated communique. I didn't want the old man getting agitated by them, and, so far, he seemed to have treated the intrusions the same way he'd brought up his four children – not worth bothering about. He was in the living room with his coat dumped on the passage floor when I closed the front door behind me. I grabbed the coat and hung it on the end of the bannister. He'd had it for fifty years – it was older than me, with much more care and attention lavished on it than he'd shown for any of his children.

'I'll put the shopping away and the food in the oven. You get settled and turn the TV on.'

His favourite game show was about to start, which meant the sound on the set would be loud enough to bother the Devil. I'd been back in the family home for a month, and every night it was like being at a Motörhead concert. I wasn't sure how long my hearing would last. Or my sanity.

I switched the oven on to warm it up and emptied the shopping bags. A man in his nineties would eat little to nothing if left on his own. I'd bought a four-pint carton of milk because his doctor had told him he needed calcium for his bones, though he knew it was too late for that. A fall two months ago had broken his hip, and now there was a piece of metal inside him to join the shrapnel acquired in France seventy years before. I placed three packets of cup-a-soup into the cupboard, opened the fridge for the corned beef, and washed the grapes. It was a measly haul for anyone to eat, which is why I'd bought us fish and chips as well.

'Food of the gods,' he used to tell me when I was knee-high to a grasshopper.

I slipped the food into the oven, then returned to the front door. When the messages had started not long after my return, I'd assumed it was only kids welcoming me back to the community. However, when they increased in frequency, the theme became more apparent: it was the opposite of a bizarre greeting. Coppers were not wanted here, even ex ones.

I dropped the plastic head into a plastic bag and cleaned up the mess, getting fake blood and grey mincemeat over my hands. The gloom of night had overtaken the minimal street lighting on the estate, but I sensed there were eyes on me, more than human ones: but electronic devices recording my every move.

I wondered if this was what it was like to be loved – a perverse, unnerving, unwanted love, but love nonetheless. I returned inside and dumped the bag into the bin. Once I'd washed my hands, I took the food out of the oven, warming my hands as I put it on plates and brought it into the living room.

The sound blared from the TV as I entered, so much I had to raise my voice to be heard.

'Do you want a drink?'

It was a stupid question. Since I was a child in this house – my parents moved here when I was two – I'd never known him to go a day without alcohol. My mother told me he hadn't touched a drop before he joined the army, but he'd made up for it since.

He was motionless in the chair, worrying me he'd slipped into one of his fugue states. His doctor had warned me they were becoming more frequent, those periods where he would forget who and where he was, gazing into space. I wondered if he'd forgotten how badly he'd treated his wife and children, and now, when he stared at me as an adult, he was in a different life.

His eyes were fixed on mine, staring at me from the

same unemotional face I'd known for forty-five years. I'd seen him angry twice, turning gammon-faced as he'd raged at my mother, but that was it. It wasn't a long stare, his interest in me evaporating in a second as he turned his gaze back to the TV and a group of people pushing plastic coins over the edge of a moving construct. The money tumbled down to another level and pushed more coins around. I remembered playing such a game as a kid at the seaside, amazed now that someone had converted it into prime time entertainment.

Motion flickered inside his eyes. 'Get me a cider.'

I went to the kitchen for two cans since I couldn't let him drink on his own. When I returned, the game show had finished, but the noise was just as loud from an old black and white cowboy movie.

I pulled up a small table and placed his fish and chips in front of him. Cider lingered on his mouth, the reflection of the TV flickering inside his eyes. Perhaps it was the only life there. I retreated to the sofa, the hot plate warming my legs, the sounds of cowboys shooting each other bouncing off the walls. He must have watched the same movie dozens of times over the years. I glanced at him funnelling fish between his lips, noticing him mouthing the dialogue from the film as he ate. Was this what I had to look forward to?

An hour later, I took him upstairs to bed. When I'd first returned to the family home – to his house, as he kept reminding me – I mentioned converting the back room into a bedroom so he needn't struggle up the stairs every night; but he wouldn't have it.

'I won't be dying in there.'

His withered frame was tiny in the large bed he'd once shared with my mother. That was before she left him after thirty years of a relationship colder than the iceberg which sank the *Titanic*. It was an image I always associated with him: a human iceberg; a man whose true self was only thirty per cent above water, the rest concealed from everyone else. Maybe it was even hidden from him.

His snoring was as loud as the TV as I went to my room. There were three bedrooms in the house, and I'd chosen the smallest because it was the one I'd had when I was a kid, where I'd locked myself away and withdrawn into my world of books, movies, and music. The posters had been removed from the walls a long time ago, but some of my books were still there; an old copy of *Dune* was the highlight, surrounded by other science fiction and horror novels from the sixties and the seventies.

Voices slipped into my room from beyond the wall, reminding me of my childhood. When I'd first moved into this bedroom – my brother had been upgraded to the bigger room when my older sisters left home, so I got his – I'd been convinced it was haunted. So every night, I'd pull the covers over my head as the voices drifted out of the wall and seemed to taunt me.

It was only after two weeks of this that I mustered up the courage to tell my mother. Her laughter filled the house as she slapped her side and told me the truth – the voices were filtering in from next door, from the room connected to mine by a thin slice of stone.

Now, I placed my ear to the wallpaper and listened, hearing muffled sounds increasing in velocity: two people arguing. These neighbours differed from my childhood, a man and a woman about a decade younger than me. I'd seen them in passing, the misery imprinted over their faces like tattoos. As the noise died down, I slipped back on to the bed, leaving their whispers to settle into the ether like ghosts.

The headphones were in my ears as I searched through my phone for music to send me to sleep. Would it be something new to guide me towards a better future or a delve into my past to live my life all over again through nostalgia and the misty-eyed memories of an existence that never happened? I settled on some contemporary minimalist electronic tunes as the soundtrack of my current plight.

The plink plonk of keyboards must have done the trick as I woke up in the early hours with a desperate need for the toilet. It was only when I'd finished pissing, stepping out to make my way back to my bedroom, that I noticed the piece of paper hanging halfway through the letterbox downstairs.

I could have left it there, but was intrigued why someone would do such a thing at night. Perhaps it was another welcome message to me from the locals. I crept down the stairs in my bare feet, my toes curling against a carpet as old as me.

My knees creaked as I bent to get the paper. I unfolded it and read the three sentences.

Meet me tomorrow at the train station at one o'clock. I'll be on platform two. It's important for your family.

I returned to bed and reread it.

It's important for your family.

I dropped it to the floor. Everyone in this house was my family, and I wasn't too keen on either of us.

Nothing was important anymore.

And I didn't think it would be ever again.

2 MYSTERY TRAIN

It was a small train station, but was busy for a Saturday afternoon. I'd left the old man at home watching the racing – gambling was always his favourite thing, but now he only watched and never fluttered. I'd arrived thirty minutes earlier than the appointed time with my mystery person.

The air was crisp, filled with the smell of lavender vape smoke. Some patrons had dumped plastic cups on the benches, pale items which would take longer to decompose than their corpses. There was a new bike stand in the far corner, but most of its rows were empty. I strode by it and went through the subway and across the other side for Platform Two. It was unoccupied, the next train to the beach twenty minutes away.

I plugged the headphones into my mobile and selected a random playlist. While I checked the latest football news online, the Lizard King was warbling about cars hissing by. A thin man overwhelmed with shopping bags was the first to join me on the platform. He stumbled up the steps and dropped half of his purchases.

Cheap frozen meals constructed from the worst ingredients tumbled from his haul, mixed in with a two-litre bottle of Lucozade and about a thousand packets of pickled onion Monster Munch. I removed a plug from my ears, *The Crystal Ship* sailing through my head, and helped him.

The chicken hot pot meal for one was cold and damp to the touch, and I wondered if he'd get these to his freezer before they melted. He gave me a grin wide enough for me to see his mouth was missing half its teeth, and of those left, there were more dark than light ones.

'Thanks, big man.'

It was an expression most people used when meeting me for the first time. My physique was one thing I hadn't inherited from my parents. When I reached fourteen, I was over six feet tall and weighed a hundred and eighty pounds. My body was muscular even before I started working out, but once I hit the gym, I was a walking advert for a teenage Conan the Barbarian. I was built to join the military, but when somebody mentioned it to my father, he'd roll his eyes, and I assumed it was his way of saying, 'Don't do it.'

So I joined the police instead.

I'd still be there twenty-five years later if I hadn't done something stupid.

The shopping man retreated into the waiting room as the platform filled up. I slipped on to a bench and scanned the latest news. The government had promised to borrow billions after slamming their predecessors for doing the same. A bloke who drove over a tent at a campsite killing a woman was sentenced to eight years in prison. Which meant he'd be out in four, possibly three, while the victim's loved ones would endure a life sentence there was no release from. Climate change protesters were arrested after painting several buses yellow in the capital. There was more bombing in the Middle East. The Royal Family were complaining about press intrusion by giving interviews to certain sections of the media.

I was reading the sports section when a shadow fell across me. One o'clock was here, and I'd hardly noticed. I slipped the phone into my pocket and peered at the person standing over me. She was tall, willowy, wearing a floral dress, a large floppy hat, and fashionable sunglasses. Her clothes were perfect for a summer's day at the beach, but even with the headwear and glasses, I recognised her: the woman from the other side of my bedroom wall. She dropped a piece of paper into my lap and turned towards the approaching train.

It fell to the ground as I stood. I picked it up and read it.

Get on the train before me. I'll sit behind you. Don't turn around or speak. No one can see us together.

Thankfully, there was no instruction to destroy the message by eating it. Instead, I put it into my pocket and walked towards the end of the platform as the train arrived. The rest of the people scampered for its two carriages.

The doors opened and passengers got off, forcing their way through those waiting to board. A young woman on crutches struggled to make her way to the front. A group of drunk young blokes blocked her by either accident or design. I cracked my knuckles, staring at them until they parted like the Red Sea. She smiled at me as the conductor helped her aboard. I got on and sat a few seats from her. The drunks headed to the other carriage.

A hiss announced the doors closing, and the metal wheels chugged slowly at first before picking up speed. As I peered out the window, watching the town disappear as industry belched out chemical vapour towards the football stadium, we left the station. The sounds of excited kids and weary adults filled every seat. The one next to me stayed empty and I assumed my significant, hulking presence had deterred most people.

Someone sat behind me. I didn't turn around but glanced into the window, hoping to see a reflection buried inside the sight of the local port outside. The journey should only take ten minutes, but time wasn't on my mind as she leant in close to my neck.

'We can't talk here.' Her voice was a whisper slithering into my ear, a plume of mystery and suspense, making me wonder what her aim was. She smelt of jasmine and it was like having my brain buried inside a bunch of flowers. 'When the train stops, get off and head towards the sea. There are some benches near the pier; take one, and I'll meet you there.'

I didn't respond, observing her in the reflection. A month after leaving London, four weeks since my resignation; this was the first time I'd felt alive on my return north. The kids got more excited as the industry disappeared, the redundant steelworks standing like a dinosaur. The scenery changed from concrete and metal to water and grass in the region's only nature reserve.

The sight of the steelworks, with its monstrous pipes spread over a once fertile land like a spider's web, brought the image of my father back to me. He'd worked in those buildings for forty years, fighting through hot steel and steam before returning to his family, usually via a trip to the bookies and then the pub. He'd only step into the house when he was hungry, leaving a mess in the kitchen for one of his kids to clean up. My mother was sleeping off a busy day by then. Should it have been a surprise to us that neither of them had any energy for their children?

My sisters escaped first because they were older. Mary

bolted to the navy. Colleen met a young man who swept her off her feet and to the other end of the country. Then there was Tommy and me, running away in different directions.

Why would four kids be so desperate to get away from their parents?

That thought was me trying to reconcile their behaviour with reason and excuses. However, even when retirement was forced upon him, the old man continued to spend little time at home; his life was watching different horses losing the money he should have been spending on us or drowning his sorrows in the local pub.

In the early days of council estates built for the workers, it must have seemed a great idea to give the working man – and it was always for men – somewhere they could relax after a hard day's slog down the pit or pushing hot metal around while trying to avoid the sting of toxic chemicals. But it can't have been too long before the drinking became more than relaxation; before the illegal gambling drifted into the dark corners of the pub, and alcohol was more of a way of life than being with your family.

Did I learn anything from being with him in that house? Was I a pillar of respectability when I moved to London and joined the force? Did my wife have a better time with her husband than my mother did with my father?

All of this rolled around inside my head as the train pulled into the station. I glanced into the window, but my mystery neighbour was already gone. Perhaps I'd dreamt the whole thing and this was a figment of my stressed imagination.

I rose with the rest of the crowd, shuffling behind people whose lives appeared to be much more exciting than mine. The smell of the sea hit me as I stepped off the train, saltwater mixing in with the aroma from the fish and chip shops decorating the road opposite the beach. I let the kids scamper before me as I headed into town. I didn't look behind me, didn't seek the woman who'd intrigued me enough to make this trip.

Shops were on either side as I strode through the centre; most were closed, the storefronts looking as if they'd been boarded up for years. Some of them had fake fronts, where it appeared as if they were a trendy bookstore or hipster bar, but they were as empty as the eyes of most locals trudging around me.

Charity shops and pubs were the predominant businesses. People could get themselves a new set of old clothes before sipping cheap booze and munching on the least appetising cuisine this side of an overflowing rubbish bin.

The seagulls led me towards the beach, a murmuration of them swooping, swerving, and diving above me as my guides. Kids with plastic buckets and spades teemed on to the sand, but there were no brave souls ready to take a dip into the sea.

Those benches she'd mentioned were on my right. I headed to them and took the first empty spot. The wood was spattered with fret, and faded illegible names were scratched into the surface near my legs.

Then she was next to me.

'Can I look at you?' I said.

Her voice was velvet rubbed against silk. 'You've seen me before.'

I turned to her; the hat and sunglasses were gone, replaced with dark, short bobbed hair and eyes bluer than the sea near us.

'You live next door to my father.'

'My name is Dolores Cook. My husband, George, and I have lived there for ten years.'

I opened my lips a little. Not quite a smile, but enough to show her I was interested: but in what?

'Why couldn't you talk to me at the house?'

Her hands trembled as she wiped at her forehead.

'Nobody talks to coppers on the estate; you get your legs broken that way.'

'I haven't been a copper for at least a month.'

She shook her head. 'It doesn't matter; even ex-coppers are *personae non gratae* on the Hills and all the other estates.' She bit at her nails. 'I don't know what it was like for you living there twenty years ago, but, like all the others, it's a law unto itself now.'

'Twenty-five years ago.'

'What?'

'I left twenty-five years ago.'

She moved a hair from her eye and touched her knee next to mine.

'Did you come back to look after your dad?'

'I don't know what I'm going to do.' It was true. I'd run back there, the place I said I'd never return to, as soon as things got tricky for me. She fluttered her eyelids. I didn't mind the flirting, but I needed to know why she'd called me here. It wasn't because she fancied me. 'Why am I here, Dolores?'

She put her hand on my leg and squeezed it. 'I need you to save my life, Frank.'

3   ECHO BEACH

I left her hand on my leg. The wind ruffled her peek-a-boo hairstyle so it flopped across her face, doing nothing for my throbbing chest.

'How am I going to save your life?'

The cerulean blue of her eyes sucked the breath from my lungs. She got up and walked to the wall near us. It wasn't much of a barrier to the occasional devastating effects of the North-Sea, doing more to obscure the view than protect people and property. She gazed at the horizon with her back to me. I could have left then, but I joined her to stare at the wind farms peering at us like mythical giants ready to storm the town. I glanced at the kids and adults building sandcastles. Somewhere in the distance, music blared from one of the many amusement arcades.

Dolores rolled up her sleeves. 'These are some of the latest things he's given me.'

Deep purple bruises dotted the skin on both arms. She leant in close, her jasmine perfume invading my senses. It was a rich bouquet forming a mallet to thump along the insides of my skull.

'Who did this to you?' I had a good idea, but I wanted her to say it.

She turned her face from mine. 'He wasn't always like this.' A heavy sigh drifted from her lips. 'Things were great up to when we got married, but they went downhill after that.'

'You should go to the police.'

Her laugh was slow and weary. 'Things don't work like that here, Frank.'

The breeze blew hair across her eye, and in that instant, she transformed into Veronica Lake, transporting me into a black and white frame from one of those old movies my father loved. Against my better judgement, I reached out and pushed the hair from her face. Her skin was warm and I got another blast of perfume to distract me.

'What do you mean?'

'Parish Hills and the surrounding estates are different places to what you knew growing up there.'

'As kids, we thought it was such a posh sounding name, Parish Hills, wondering what must have happened to all the toffs and their big houses before we were born.' A blast of memory returned to me and I forgot about her bruises for a second. 'Some kid at school told me they'd been destroyed in the war, but I knew the estate was built after that. We only ever called it the Hills, even though it's as flat as a pancake.'

'At least that hasn't changed.'

Somehow the mood had shifted, and now it was as if we were a couple enjoying a day at the seaside. I reached into my pocket for the packet of cigarettes that wasn't there anymore. I'd chewed the gum, tried the patches and even those awful vapes, but it was never the same. I imagined an invisible stick of poison between my lips, dragging on it as I thought of what to say to her.

'Why can't you go to the police?'

She inched closer to me. 'All the estates look after themselves, and some woman beaten up by her husband isn't high on the agenda.'

None of what she said was making sense. 'How do they do this?'

Dolores looked at me as if I was an ancient artefact dredged up from the seabed.

'Back in your day, did you have coppers patrolling the community?'

I took a drag on my imaginary cigarette. 'Not only did we have a Beat Bobby on the streets, but there was also a local police station near our house.'

I remembered the outside of it, with its blue façade and twinkling lights straight out of an old British movie. I ended up inside it on more than one occasion, chastised by coppers who appeared to have more important things to do than deal with kids throwing stones at trains or nicking glue from some poor shopkeeper.

'Well, all those local stations are gone, and the cuts in police numbers mean you're more likely to see a dinosaur wandering the streets than someone crossing over the thin blue line.' She glanced at the seagulls overhead. 'And that's just what certain people wanted; it gave them the opportunity they craved.'

'You're talking about organised criminals?'

I'd seen it plenty of times down south: a set of circumstances would lead to the authorities – the police, the council, social services, even religious groups – disappearing from communities and being replaced by those with less than altruistic motives for taking control and offering protection to certain areas. It wasn't a breakdown in law and order as much as a replacement by people more than willing to live and work on the other side of the divide. But it meant a lot of ordinary up-standing citizens would get sucked into a way of life they had no chance of avoiding.

Or escaping from.

'They see themselves more as guardians of the community than petty criminals.'

'But crime still happens, and it's unreported?'

She shrugged. 'Such is life.'

'And these people won't help you with your husband?'

'George is too much of a cash cow for them to interfere with that because of me.'

'How does that work?'

'He has his own taxi, so he drops stuff off and picks things up for them all the time. He's a valuable commodity in the local economy; that's what he keeps on telling me.'

Her laugh wasn't one of happiness.

'Go to the police. Show them your bruises and tell them what you've told me.'

'I'll get worse than these bruises if I do that; you don't talk to the coppers in the Hills or the other estates.' Fear rippled through her, and I recalled the pig's head on the doorstep yesterday. How long would it be before someone banged on the door and told me in no uncertain terms to leave? 'I just need you to scare him for me.'

'I can't do that, Dolores. I'm not a copper anymore.'

She grabbed my hands before I could react. 'But you were a coper and one of the best. It's criminal, pardon the pun, what they did to you. You gave them twenty-five years of your life. You get that scumbag Matthews to confess to his murders and show you where the bodies are buried, and then they kick you out. It's a disgrace.'

Her knowledge of the last days of my career was impressive, though not accurate. The touch of her skin was intoxicating enough for me to push aside the disappointment of what had happened in London; instead, I focused on the simple facts.

'I was charged with gross misconduct, Dolores; maybe you shouldn't be relying on someone like me to help you. If you won't speak to the police, then go to social services.'

She pulled away from me, anger flaring out of her eyes and across her face. There was an intensity there, burning brighter than the sun and scorching my cheeks.

'You'd break the law to help a dead woman, but not me?'

'I didn't break the law, and I am trying to help you.'

'I've heard all the stories, read the posts on the internet.' She'd changed from a vulnerable, desperate individual to a fury of resentment and irritation. 'You got him to confess to the last murder and show you where the bodies were buried in the woods, and everyone knows how you did it.'

I slumped against the wall, wondering where the nearest shop was so I could buy twenty Benson and Hedges, not even sure if that brand still existed or if it was only the smoke and mirrors of some dim and distant memory.

'And how did I do that, Dolores?'

'You threatened his family; you pushed his head into the river and held him there until you knew he'd have to confess. You made him show you where those poor women were buried; you brought some relief to their families. You put a serial killer behind bars. They should have given you a medal, not forced you out.'

Only some of what she said was true. I stopped myself from mentioning that if I hadn't left the force and run from

London to return north, she wouldn't be with me now asking for help.

'I never touched Matthews or threatened him; they were things he said later to escape justice.'

I glanced at the kids on the beach and wondered, not for the first time, why I'd never wanted a family.

Then I remembered the old man sitting in his chair and knew why.

'Is that true?'

I peered across the sea. 'Matthews had already been cautioned twice when I took him to the woods. I should have done it again. I should also have reiterated he had the right to speak to a solicitor. However, I didn't do any of those things. Instead, we shared cigarettes and talked about his life.'

She was gripped now with the tale of my self-destruction.

'So, what happened?'

'We were there for four hours, my uniformed officers waiting in the car on the ridge behind us. Matthews loved every minute of it, talking to someone like me when we were so close to where he'd buried his victims.' The invisible nicotine burnt the back of my throat. 'He'd been killing for years, had studied forensics so he could cover his tracks, and then I got lucky on that day.'

'Lucky, how?'

'After all that time, in that situation, something must have worn away at him. Maybe it was guilt. Perhaps it was the realisation of his terrible crimes: three murders which we know of, at least another four more I'm convinced he's responsible for. It was the perfect mix of the right time in the right place in the right set of circumstances. He confessed to the last murder and showed me where he'd buried three of his victims. Of course, later, when he denied it all and made those claims, he couldn't be charged with that one, but there was enough forensic evidence – ironically since he'd done so much to eradicate it – to sentence him for life.'

'And for you to lose your job.'

I moved from the wall and threw the imaginary ciggie into the sea.

'It was worth it to put him away and tell the families what had happened to their loved ones.'

Dolores strode past me, the smell of her perfume lingering in the air. She was only a few feet away when she peered straight into my eyes.

'You gave up your career and your life for the dead, but for me, you'll do nothing.' I didn't know what to say. 'What will you do, Frank, when you hear my screams from the other side of the wall?'

4 TRAIN IN VAIN

Kids scattered around me as she disappeared from view. Their cries of happiness and joy were loud and unruly, but they couldn't drown out her voice echoing inside my skull.

What will you do, Frank, when you hear my screams from the other side of the wall?

A group of pensioners, struggling to eat their ice creams as the wind whipped around them, shuffled past me as I slapped my head to get Dolores out of it. Her words lingered in my mind, wrapped in the smell of her perfume and the touch of her skin.

And I could still see those bruises.

I pushed my fingers into my forehead, rubbing at my skin, hearing her in my mind. Her voice mixed in with the grey tones of Christopher Matthews bragging to me, enjoying himself as he told me every terrible detail of his crimes. If a smile could be described as evil, that's how Matthews looked to me at his trial, the crooked corners of his lips seeming to turn into horns. But that was only

because I'd been overworked and hadn't slept for two days –
the police therapist made me realise that.

But I still had Matthews's last words stuck to my brain.

*Never wrestle with pigs, Frank. You both get dirty and
the pig likes it.*

I'd believed it was another dig at me being a copper –
not that I would be for much longer after that trial – but the
more the words echoed inside my mind, the more I thought
they meant something else.

I shook my head, sending Christopher Matthews's grinning face slinking back into the shadows, and I pictured
Dolores again. I was in no hurry to follow her to the train
station. A day at the seaside would do me some good. I
headed into the town centre, where the shops lived a life
that appeared to be as perilous as my current state of mind.
For every one open, at least two others had been boarded
up. The council had tried their best to make these dead
retail outfits appear part of a thriving economic setting.
Instead of the old, rusty nail-encrusted wooden boards
you'd expect for a failed business venture, someone had
come up with the bright idea of prettifying them with a fake
front. Now they didn't look like empty shells for desperate
rats and last year's rubbish because the outsides were plas-
tered with images of things not real, of people who only
existed in glossy advertising magazines and photoshoots and
who'd never travelled this far north before. Their hair and
skin were perfect, their smiles wide and beaming as they
pretended to drink wine, cook vegetables, or read a book:
three things the region was not renowned for. You'd be
classed as strange around here if you drank anything which
wasn't beer or cheap spirits, while the locals would peer at
you as if you were a visitor from outer space for eating something that wasn't a fried dead animal. And reading was rare

unless the material contained a pair of bare female breasts on page three or the racing forecasts.

A group of kids scampered past me, pretending to be characters from the *Star Wars* movies while shouting at each other in Arabic. It made me smile, and I forgot about Dolores and her parting words. Perhaps I'd bring the old man out here, get the sun on his head and the sea breeze into his lungs. It might do him some good, and at least he'd be out of that house.

Then I thought of Dolores again and wondered if I should ask my father if he knew anything of what she'd claimed. And if he did, would he remember it?

And what would I do about it?

Music was playing somewhere ahead of me, some old rock-and-roll tune blaring out of an ice cream parlour. But I couldn't take the old man there since he didn't like ice cream and hated all popular music.

The sun washed over the town as I continued my walkabout. A bakery on my left was selling out-of-date food to a queue of customers keen for a bargain: a withered old man, dressed as if he was going to a 1940s wedding in his faded suit, light-blue shirt and white tie, grasped what looked like the last of his wife's jewellery in his eager hands. Behind him were identical twin girls in matching shirts and skirts scooping up what day-old pastries they could find. They grinned at me in unison as I kept on walking.

Next was a used record store of the type I'd frequented every weekend during my teenage years. Its doors were flung open and experimental electronic sounds drifted out to startle a confused gathering of tourists and residents in equal measure.

I'd had nothing to eat since leaving the house and a smaller, more irritable version of me was clawing at my insides. So I searched for the nearest café and settled on the first greasy spoon I found, though that was doing grease a considerable disservice. The atmosphere cooled as I went inside, which I assumed was because most people hadn't seen someone as tall as me close up before. Then most of them smirked as I banged my head on a low-hanging light, or maybe I was just too big for this establishment. So there I was, out-of-place once again.

It was the type of joint that attracted the dregs of society, who were trying to suck out the last bit of taste from day-old coffee. There was a free table in the corner with a nice window view of the outside world. A tall blonde server tottered over on high heels the Surgeon General should have condemned.

'What can I get ya, love?'

I didn't need to scan the menu. 'I'll have a full English breakfast, please.'

I could already taste the bacon and sausage as she glared at me. Her glasses were about to plummet from her nose until she pushed them back up.

'Breakfasts stop at twelve.'

She leant towards me with a cleavage desperate to burst from her top and get ahead of her like a body going over Niagara Falls. I ordered two large bacon baps. An old man in the corner hooted with laughter and grinned at me.

As I waited for the food, I settled into the uncomfortable chair, my gaze fixed on a young couple. She wouldn't have looked out of place in a *Vogue* catalogue, with light-brown hair tied behind her. Her paramour was one of those modern men who wore their hair long and their facial piercings even longer. There was something in his ear that wasn't a ring, but more of a sizeable dangling rectangle. You wouldn't want to get stuck behind him at an airport. Tattoos covered his arms and his neck as if ink was going out of fashion.

A bunch of beer-bellied, poorly dressed blokes staggered into the café. It was only the afternoon, but their speech was slurred and incomprehensible. They must have been regular customers because the tired-looking woman at the counter knew what they wanted regardless of their struggles to put two words together. They searched for seats and their bleary eyes found the young couple. For a split second, I saw their addled minds getting ready to hurl some abuse until, as a group, they noticed me staring at them. I didn't know who they were, but I recognised their type. They sloped into the corner like cockroaches scurrying under a fridge.

The food arrived and was good, the taste of crispy bacon covered in dollops of brown sauce warming my insides better than any sunshine could. I spent the rest of the afternoon in the café, keeping the proprietors happy by spending money on a cake which was too dry and juice that only had a passing acquaintance with any type of fruit. The young couple finished their meal and went off to enjoy the beach. The drunks mumbled and grumbled before going back to the pub.

A chill had descended on the town when I left the café, sending most other tourists and me to the train station. I decided to return soon and bring my father with me. I didn't think he'd seen a beach since Normandy. He couldn't spend hours on his feet, but perhaps I'd get a wheelchair for him. Then I'd have to talk him into letting me push him around – a strange reversal of fortune. I guess it's what happens if children stay long enough to see one or both of their parents reach that age where they need looking after. Not that I was doing it out of the goodness of my heart. I'd had nowhere to go, so had gone to the place which had never felt like a home to me.

As I made my way to the platform, I wondered if he'd ever pushed me in a pram or taken me to places like this. Of course, I had no memory of such things, but it didn't mean they hadn't happened. My mother was the one who'd looked after the children, that's what I could remember, but my childhood memories weren't many. The ones I had were hazy – the type that bordered the thin divide between what you assumed to be true and what could be a dream or an illusion.

The earliest memory I had was from around the age of five or six, a harrowing moment when I sliced my knee open on a piece of broken glass in the grounds of the power station near the house, so anything might have happened in the period leading up to that. Perhaps those early years were the best moments in my relationship with my parents, especially my father, and everything which came after them was an aberration.

Four kids left home as soon as possible, but don't all children leave their families eventually?

I stood on the platform with the train due in ten minutes. Most of the kids were drained of energy, matching the tiredness in the eyes of the surrounding adults. But it was a weariness born out of joy and good times, and it made me happy to see. It was a curious feeling, something I'd been missing all those years pursuing criminals while dealing with the incompetence of some of my colleagues. And those times when I'd had to console victims and their families: there can only be so many occasions when you look people in the eye and don't feel distraught at their agony.

The barriers came down and closed the road to traffic as

the train approached. I was about to put the seaside behind me but, as I readied to board the carriage, I promised I would return and bring the old man with me. It was the final acceptance of our role reversal.

On the journey back, I never thought of Dolores once.

5 MEMORIES

I had the mobile in my hand as I walked into the house. I was going to impress the old man by ordering a take-away online. Curry was always his favourite when I was a kid. I wasn't sure if his delicate constitution could take it now, but it was worth a go. Plus, I was convinced he wouldn't eat anything at all unless I made an effort to tempt him.

The phone nearly fell to the floor as I went into the living room. He was sitting on the carpet, gazing into a torrent of photographs in front of him. Even from a distance, I recognised the people in them: family members from down the years, some of whom were no longer with us, others I'd not seen in a long time.

He didn't realise I was there, so I coughed.

His neck creaked as he turned to me. 'What are we doing tomorrow?'

The question threw me for a second until I remembered what he meant.

'You have a doctor's appointment; they're going to take some blood.'

His arms were so thin and anaemic, it seemed impossible there was anything left in his veins.

'I never liked *Doctor Who*.' There was a spark in his voice I hadn't heard for a while. 'Your older sisters loved it when they were kids, but I could never understand the fuss. Why would you want to watch a show about alien monsters when there are plenty of real ones here?'

He picked up a photo, a tattered, grainy black-and-white image of those sisters, Mary and Colleen, who'd left home before I was born. They were both still alive; their Facebook profiles told me that. Not that I went looking for them online; one of those People You May Know notifications informed me they were still around. Curiously, they weren't Facebook Friends with each other.

'Have you been watching *Doctor Who* while I was out?'

The TV was on with the sound muted. People were cooking food for a competition in a prime-time TV spot. If you'd told me thirty years ago people would watch this type of show in their millions, I wouldn't have believed you. It was the same for competitive celebrity ballroom dancing. Not that they were celebrities I'd ever heard of. Still, it was better than watching repeats of 1970s comedy shows that weren't funny.

The old man waved a wrinkled hand at a bloke attempting to make a cake in the shape of a racing car.

'Those talking pepper pots were on again. They're so annoying.'

It was nice to see him animated, but I wasn't sure if what he'd seen had been on the TV or inside his head.

My mother used to tell me a story about Mary and *Doctor Who*. My sister must have been three or four years old when the Daleks first appeared in glorious black and white on the nation's screens. It was such a shock for little

Mary Walker that she fell from the back of the sofa where she'd been sitting. My mother would use the tale as an example of the power of TV over the minds of small children, while all I could think about was why a baby was sitting on the top of the sofa. Of course, I never got a reasonable parental answer when I asked my mother this.

I knelt close to him. 'What have you been doing?' It wasn't in me to call him Dad. I thought of him as my father, but he was never that to me. 'What's going on, Jack?'

The sound of his name sparked a response behind his tired eyes. He lifted fingers resembling ancient branches to his head.

'Sometimes I can remember it all, but then bits of it fade away.' His hand slid down his cheek. 'More and more things are leaving me.'

Sorrow engulfed me – not for this man as my father, but for him as a person. He'd had no time for me or any of his other children, but that didn't mean I had to treat him the same. I peered into the pile of memories and picked up the largest.

'Do you remember this, Jack?'

He put the picture of my sisters down and took this one in his shaky hand, the sparkle in his eyes illuminating his face. There were eight people in the photo, six adults and two children. He pointed to the tallest one.

'This is me.'

It was a much younger version of him, maybe twenty-four, with short curly hair and a smile I'd never seen recreated in real life. It was so warm, even in that faded black and white, and I wondered what had happened to it by the time I came along.

'Do you know when it was taken?'

I did, but it was a prompt to see where his memory was.

The first week I was back, I'd taken him to the hospital. He'd missed an appointment the previous month, and I only knew about it because the NHS sent him a letter; there was no phone in the house, either mobile or landline, until I got there. The appointment was for a dementia test. His GP had assessed him and then referred him to the hospital. They had given him several cognition tests, and tomorrow was a follow-up to check his blood.

I wanted to ask him questions about his neighbours, especially Dolores, but I'd decided it would be pointless with his memory being so bad. Now, with that spark in his eyes, I thought it might prove worthwhile.

'It's my wedding photograph.'

'That's right, Jack.' It was nearly seventy years old. 'Do you recognise anyone else in the photo?'

He held it in both hands, steadying it as he scrutinised its occupants. Would he recall the woman he'd pushed away?

'That's my father.' He touched the image of the man behind him. I had no idea what my paternal grandfather was called.

'Do you remember his name?'

His breathing came in short, laboured bursts, and I assumed I'd pressed him too hard. I'd heard about organisations that worked with the elderly, showing them old photographs to kick start their memories. Still, it had to be taken slowly, a few steps at a time; you couldn't draw out the past like water from a tap without the possibility of overflowing the mind.

'No, I don't.'

His voice trembled and wavered. There was a tear in his eye. I removed tissue from my pocket and wiped his face. I took the image from him and placed it back with the others.

'What we need to do is get some photo albums and sort these into chronological order.' I peered into their depths and wondered how many of me were in there. 'Are you hungry? I thought I'd get us a curry.'

His hand shook as he lifted it to his lips. 'I haven't had a curry in a long time. Can I have a cider with it?'

'Of course, Jack; maybe even two cans if you eat all your food.'

In one second, I was caught up in a role reversal returning me to my childhood and my mother telling me I couldn't have any cake if I didn't finish my Brussel sprouts. I hated sprouts with a passion, but I loved my mother's home-made cakes, especially the chocolate ones.

He peered at the photos. 'I haven't put them away.'

I pulled up one of the small tables my parents had received as a wedding present and sat on it next to him. My mother used to scold me for sitting on it when I was a kid.

'Don't worry. I'll sort them once we've ordered the food. Do you want to see how you can get a meal without leaving the house?'

He turned his gaze to the phone as I enlarged the details on the screen so he could see them.

'I'll have to get me one of these magic devices.'

The sparkle in his eyes had transformed into a grin, and his happiness made me feel good. I wasn't sure when the last time that had happened.

Maybe it never had.

'You always liked a Balti, do you remember?'

His face trembled and I thought I'd lost him again, but he surprised me once more.

'Especially with a few ciders.'

It took me ten minutes to order the food, longer than necessary, but he continued to ask me questions about the process. It had taken forty-five years to happen, but I finally had a significant moment with my father.

And all because I'd ordered a curry using my phone.

When it was done, I turned up the sound on the TV – there was a game show on somewhere – and then I collected the photos. I'd seen most of them before, but not for many years. Those of me, dressed as a cowboy or kicking a football around in the garden, made me smile. The ones of Mary and Colleen as kids or teenagers always made me feel the same way – these were people who had grown up and left home while I was still a baby. I knew as much about them and their lives as I did any stranger.

Then there were the images of Tommy. There were more of him than the other kids, peering into the camera with mischief in his eyes – especially when he had some girl on his arm.

'They'll never eat all that.'

My father's voice brought me back to the present and I put all the photos into the box, turning to see him staring at a giant cake baked in the shape of the Eiffel Tower.

Our food arrived within forty minutes. We sat and ate while he watched the TV, losing himself in some cop show from the 1970s. We drank two cans of cider each. He was ready for bed when we'd finished, so I helped him upstairs. Then I cleared everything away and flicked through the channels for something to distract my mind from the day's events.

What was there to make of the strange situation with Dolores Cook? I half expected her to bang on the door at any moment to ask for my help. But instead, I found an episode of *South Park* to fall asleep in front of; only I couldn't sleep, and that one episode turned into two, then three, and eventually four.

It was two o'clock before I climbed the stairs for bed. The old man was snoring away in the main bedroom. Was this progress in our relationship? Was the change in his behaviour down to age, his memory loss, or something else?

I slipped between the sheets and hoped to get my first decent night's rest since my mistake in London.

An hour later, I sprang awake at the sound of screams from next door. Something thumped into the wall, and I tumbled to the floor. Then the screams came again. There was no mistaking what it was, no mistaking who it was.

I was scrambling into my clothes when Dolores shrieked my name again.

I bounced off the wall and the bannister as I tumbled down the stairs, uncaring if the noise would wake the old man up. I had the door open and was outside before I realised I was only wearing a flimsy shirt and trousers. The night clawed at my skin while the cold concrete bit into my bare feet.

The noises from next door had vanished, disappeared into the silence of the street. I climbed over the small fence separating the two houses and wondered how I'd get inside without breaking in.

I didn't have to deliberate for long. The front door was open, a tiny gap between the wood showing me the light inside. I pushed it further aside and peered through the opening. I didn't call out or wait, striding into the corridor.

The house was designed the same as my father's – I'd never been able to think of it as our house or my house – but in the opposite: the rooms were all on the other side. I went into the living room. It looked as if someone had robbed the place: it was missing most of what you'd expect in a modern home – no TV, computer, or games system, no furniture apart from a tattered three-piece sofa. Holes littered the carpet and it stank of cat piss.

I exited back into the corridor and moved into the kitchen, which was equally barren. The floor was filthy, with empty pizza boxes stacked on the fridge.

I turned around and went into the dining room, though I doubt any dining had taken place in there for a long time, finding a table, two chairs, and the stink of cigarettes. Strewn across the floor were stacks of old newspapers, the local rag, and recent issues of the *Daily Mail*.

The last place to check was upstairs. I ran my fingers over the dirty paper peeling from the walls, letting the silence calm my beating heart. At the top of the stairs was a bathroom, empty apart from the stench of the unflushed toilet and a bunch of dirty clothes piled in the bathtub, followed by three bedrooms along the landing.

The main bedroom was on my left, the equivalent of where my father was likely snoring right now. I opened the door, finding it bare apart from a large unmade bed. Somebody had ripped the pillows to pieces; their insides spewed over the floor as if the furniture had thrown up, while the duvet stank of fresh vomit.

I moved towards the last two rooms. The one ahead was adjacent to my room on the other side of the wall, so it made sense for Dolores's voice to have come from there. I held my hand out flat and forced the door open.

Then George Cook's fist hit me in the head.

The speed took me by surprise and I fell into the wall. My legs buckled, and it was all he needed to rain more blows upon my shoulders and spine. He was at least a foot shorter than me and his arms were spindly. I stuck out my chest and rose, my arm out and forcing him into the bedroom.

He tumbled into the cheap stereo system, knocking CDs and records all over the place. Seven-inch singles with Cliff Richard and the Bay City Rollers on the covers were under my feet as I rushed at him. Then he brought a knife up and stabbed at me. The blade glanced off my palm, nicking the skin. I stepped towards the far wall as blood dripped from the wound.

'I'm going to slit your throat, ya bastard.'

The fear inside his eyes betrayed the arrogance in his voice. He was one of those blokes who give an air of confidence until challenged, and then fold like a cheap suit.

'Where's Dolores?'

The smell of my blood staining the carpet must have galvanised him.

'Are you the one she's been shagging?'

His grin displayed a mouth missing fifty per cent of its teeth. The stink of his halitosis was more painful than the wound in my hand.

My hands became fists at my side. 'Have you hurt her?'

His cheek wobbled with a nervous tic, the only give-away sign of intelligence lurking inside him.

'She's no concern of yours, fucker.' He waved the blade at my face. 'I'll cut you up, and then do the same to her.'

Before he'd finished, I grabbed his wrist, bending it back. The crack of his bone was the sweetest thing I'd heard all night. The second was his scream as I threw him across the bed. The knife fell to the floor and I kicked it away.

I left him there and went into the last room, the one opposite mine. She was in the corner with her face pushed up to the wall. There were scratches on her arms and legs. I couldn't tell if she was dead or alive. The window was open, the wind blowing the curtains apart as the sound of sirens headed our way.

My hand was moving to her shoulder, tension in my bones, as George returned and dragged me backwards. Then, with a surprising amount of strength for someone so skinny, he tossed me into a table and lamp. I hit them simultaneously, my head catching on the edge of the wood, cutting me above the eye. Some of my blood obscured my vision as he jumped at me. All I could think about as he ended up on my stomach was what drugs he must have taken.

His fingers dug into my throat, but the damage to my pride was more painful than what he was inflicting. I must have been out of shape if this scrawny druggie could catch me off guard. Before I could stick my nails into his flesh, other hands than mine dragged him off me. Blood slipped into my eyes as I gazed at the boys and girls in blue. Then they turned from me and went to Dolores.

I stuck my hands into the carpet and pushed my aching limbs up. When I stood and wiped my face, I saw a room full of uniformed coppers. One of them was babbling something at me, but the ringing in my ears translated what he said into the dialogue from a *Tom and Jerry* cartoon.

'What?' I mumbled.

I held out my hand as if seeking their help, but all they did was slap a pair of handcuffs on me. This wasn't how I'd expected my night to end. Then my hearing sprang back to life like when your ears pop after getting off a plane.

'You're coming with us, sonny.'

The young bloke in the blue uniform must have been half my age and size, but I didn't resist. I led him downstairs, happy to see Dolores alive and speaking to a female officer. Then the copper bundled me outside. I planted my feet into the ground, and the poor bloke snapped back like a broken elastic band.

'I'll go with you, but I have to make sure my father is okay.' I nodded towards the house. 'He's ninety-three and in ill health. If he wakes up to find me gone, he'll panic.'

I doubt he'd ever worried about any of his kids, but there was always a first time for everything. The copper stared at me as if I'd spoken a different language.

'Do you live next door, sir?'

The police officer I'd seen talking to Dolores was now speaking to me.

'I do. My name is Frank Walker, and that's my father's house.'

The first officer handed me over to her.

'It'll be best if you go in and tell him.' She smiled at me warmly enough to light up a cold night. 'He'll probably freak out if he wakes up with me standing over him.'

I could think of a lot worse things to happen. 'Thanks, Officer...?'

The smile disappeared as quickly as it had come.

'You don't need to know my name, sir.'

She climbed over the fence and waited for me to do the same. I followed suit and went into the house, with her just behind me.

'He's asleep upstairs,' I said to her.

'Are you sure?' She pointed to the light in the living room.

I used my shoulder to get inside, shocked to see him sitting in his pyjamas in his usual chair. He gazed at me, appearing more alive than I'd seen him in the month I'd been there. His lips trembled as he spoke.

'You wouldn't expect me to sleep with all that noise coming from next door. What were you doing in there?'

I looked at the copper, and then back at him.

'Mrs Cook needed some help; that's why I was there.'

'We're taking your son to the station to give us a statement, Mr Walker. Will you be okay on your own for a while?'

He rolled his eyes at her. 'Of course I'll be fine. I've got by without him all these years, haven't I?'

She didn't answer, and neither did I. We left him sitting there as he fumbled for the TV remote. There was an ambulance outside the house with EMTs attending to Dolores and George. The officer's hand was on my back as she guided me out.

'We need to get your cut sorted before going to the station.'

I shrugged. I was in no hurry. I tried to catch Dolores's attention, but an EMT took her and the husband into the ambulance. Another EMT came over and spent five minutes patching me up.

Then the copper put me into the back of a police car, its flashing yellow lights hurting my eyes. She got into the front and one of her colleagues drove us away. I twisted my neck to glance at the ambulance as we left.

'Someone needs to watch the husband. I went into the house to help Dolores because he assaulted her.'

The female officer looked at me. 'That's not what she said. She's claiming you broke in and attacked them both.'

The pain in my head increased a thousandfold.

7 WATCHING THE DETECTIVES

The police car stank of fresh vomit and testosterone. I couldn't appreciate the irony of my reversal of fortune, trying to forget the number of times I'd been in the front with the suspected criminal in the back.

Is that what I was now, a suspected criminal? Why had Dolores accused me of attacking her? Surely, it was just confusion, or perhaps the officer misheard her? No, they would have asked her more than once. I should have been worried, but I let the journey wash over me.

We travelled in complete silence, leaving the Hills and driving through the next estate, exotically named the Northern Quarter, even though I was sure it was in the southern part of town. We skirted around the edge of the centre before heading under the central rail line, going over the Border, so-called because it separated the council estates from the rougher parts of the town when I was a kid.

The police station was ahead of us. It wasn't the one I was dragged into when I was fourteen for shoplifting, which had long since been demolished. Instead, this was one of those modern buildings full of bright colours and angled brickwork. It looked like a giant Rubik's Cube God had tossed to the side once it proved too challenging to complete.

The car park was empty apart from three vehicles – which wasn't unusual considering it was four in the morning – as the officers frog-marched me into the station. The lights were subdued and it was short on personnel, only two uniformed officers and a striking-looking woman in a smart suit sitting at a desk. She glanced up at us as one of my guards signed paperwork at reception.

'Bring him here, Jules.'

Her voice was full of weariness, her eyes fading with the artificial light above her.

'He's all yours, DI Rose.' Jules seemed disappointed to be losing custody of me. 'Though I can handle this if you want?'

The detective inspector stared at me as I glanced at the nametag on her desk. 'I need something to keep me awake.' Jules unlocked my cuffs and walked away. DI Sara Rose continued to peer right through me. 'I don't know who's the more surprised, Mr Walker, you or I.'

I rubbed at the marks on my wrists.

'They called ahead and told you who they were bringing in?'

She glanced at a piece of paper on her desk.

'When the alleged victim, Dolores Cook, informed my colleagues who you are, they had no choice but to let me know. We don't get many celebrities here.'

I ignored the jab and stared at the small replica ship near her hand. It was the *MV Empire Windrush*.

'You think I'm surprised to see a woman of Caribbean descent rise to a senior position in the British police.'

Her laugh was infectious. 'I'd hardly say being a DI is a

senior position.' She peered at the paper again. 'In your twenty-five years in the police, Mr Walker, how many female officers from ethnic minority backgrounds did you encounter?'

'Perhaps a dozen.'

'Women of colour make up less than two per cent of the force, so I guess I am the exception, especially up here.'

'You know about my background?'

'I've just spent fifteen minutes on the phone speaking to one of your colleagues.' She shook her head. 'Sorry, ex-colleagues. I think they miss you down there.'

'Is that why I'm talking to you and not a uniform?'

Her expression changed in an instant. 'According to our witnesses, you entered their house uninvited and attacked both of them.'

The accusation was too stupid to respond to, but I had no choice.

'And why would I do that?'

She glanced at that paper again, but I assumed all the information was in her head.

'The husband claims you were having an affair with his wife before she ended it. You were upset, stormed in and attacked them.'

'What about the bruises on her body? They are weeks old.'

'Can I call you Frank?' She pushed the paper to the side and didn't wait for a reply. 'We take all allegations of violence seriously, plus we had officers on the scene during your confrontation with Mr Cook.' Her gaze lingered on me. 'But he has a rap sheet longer than your arm, including making false accusations against police officers, so I take his claims with a pinch of salt. Mrs Cook's words are another matter entirely.'

I told her the story of the note and our trip to the coast, then hearing the noises from next door.

'I couldn't just leave her like that when she was screaming.'

'How did you get inside?'

'The door was open.'

'You're still playing the Good Samaritan, then?'

'I won't ignore someone in trouble.'

'So you're sticking to that story?'

'Shouldn't you be writing this down or typing it into a computer?'

She scrutinised my face as if I was a failed exhibit in a museum.

'Why did you do it?'

'I told you, I never touched Dolores. I don't know why she's lying, but she is.'

'That's not what I'm talking about.' She lifted a pen from the desk and pressed it to her lips. 'With all your experience, with twenty-five years on the job, including the capture of two other serial killers, the arrest of the Camden Canal rapist, and shutting down numerous trafficking and drugs gangs, why did you do what you did with Christopher Matthews at the river?'

This change of tack from the present to the past confused me. Perhaps it was the lack of sleep. Or this was her tactic to catch me off guard and in a lie.

'I don't know what you mean, Inspector Rose.'

She rolled the pen between her fingers, manipulating it like an amateur conjurer.

'You ignored protocol, specifically PACE. You knew what you were doing and recognised it would have serious consequences for both of you. The more I think about it, the more I consider you did it on purpose, pushing the self-destruct button. And if you'll do that once, you might again.'

The breath escaped from me in slow, shallow gasps. She wasn't the first person to ask me this, and, like with the others, I had no urgency to answer, but I gave her part of the truth.

'I could see it in his eyes when I walked him down to the river. There was something desperate to get out of him, and this was my only chance to discover where he'd buried the bodies. Breaching Code C of the Police and Criminal Evidence Act never crossed my mind when I spotted the opportunity to get the truth from him.'

She peered into my eyes. 'You befriended him?'

I shook my head. 'We all need a connection in life, DI Rose, to find at least one person we can open up to and reveal what we keep hidden. That's what I saw burning inside of him – his need to connect, to unburden himself to another human being. I had to reach out to him, but not as a copper. If I'd read him his rights, then the moment would've been lost. He'd have been back in the middle of a police investigation and his defence mechanism would've kicked in. So I made a choice and, given a chance to go back to it, I'd do the same again.'

She leant into her seat and studied me, the pen now discarded on the desk.

'You lived in London for twenty-five years, longer than you lived in your home town. Do you feel like a stranger returning here?'

I was tired and she knew it, could probably see it in my face. What she was doing, switching from what happened with Dolores and her husband to my recent past, didn't fool me. She was trying to establish my state of mind as I entered that house – did my previous behaviour mean I was erratic enough to do what Dolores claimed?

'It doesn't matter where you live, Inspector Rose; it's only a place.'

'I disagree, Frank. The house you grew up in has all kinds of memories buried in it: the dishes you ate off; the funny old way a door creaks; the hours you spent reading in your favourite chair – those all meant one thing in the past, but take on new significance when you encounter them again. There is a reason we treasure heirlooms. Perhaps after your recent traumatic experiences in London, you came home seeking comfort in your past. Then you met the neighbour and she smiled at you, a woman a lot younger than you. That's bound to make any bloke feel good about himself, never mind one who's going through a low period. But then she ends it and all your disappointments come crashing back like a hurricane, blowing away your positive emotions to be replaced by anger and frustration. That's when you went next door and attacked them.'

She leant back into her chair with a satisfied grin, making her look like an amateur psychologist.

'That's a nice theory, DI Rose, but it's all total bollocks.'

She shook her head and laughed.

'So why did you return after so long away? Was it to look after a father you hadn't seen for over two decades?'

Now that was a good question. I glanced at the model of the *Windrush* again.

'I needed a change of scene. I doubt I'll be staying here permanently.'

Did that depend on my father or me?

She grabbed the pen and wrote something on the paper in front of her.

'Well, make sure you don't go anywhere soon, not

without informing us first. We still need to get this situation sorted.'

'Aren't you going to charge me with anything? I'm surprised you haven't recorded any of this conversation.'

She looked around the room before coming back to me.

'How many staff do you see in here, Frank?'

I guessed this was another one of her psychological games examining the state of my mind, but I played along anyway.

'Including you, there are four.'

She smiled at my skill in basic maths.

'That's correct. You probably think it's not a bad work-force considering we're a provincial northern police force, and it's the early hours of the morning in midweek, but come eight o'clock, there might be twenty people working here, and that will include the admin.' She held up her hands. 'We don't have the staff to do everything we need. Cuts in numbers and the closure of over half the region's stations have left us teetering on a crisis that could happen at any moment. As serious as Mrs Cook's allegation is against you, there's something in her words and her husband's past behaviour that bothers me, not to mention your exemplary record. All this tells me we must dig a little deeper before making this official and committing ourselves to unnecessary hours of paperwork.'

I didn't complain about her laissez-faire attitude, but I found it curious.

'If the public finds out, won't they freak out?'

'What, you mean if the media run a story about a disgraced ex-copper hitting a woman, and then being let off by the police?'

'I wasn't disgraced.'

'It doesn't matter; that's what the media will go with.

Most people won't read beyond the headline and the first paragraph. Some of them might dig further into your past, resurrecting other scandals.'

'What other scandals?' A volcano erupted inside my head.

She pretended to glance at the paper again.

'Well, there's your wife leaving you for one.'

I dug my nails into the arms of the chair.

'We're divorced and she returned to India. Most of her family are there.'

'Apart from you.'

'I'm not her family.'

Not anymore.

'You were married at twenty, not long after you met her in London, and divorced five years ago.' She stared right into me. It was a piercing gaze that made her eyes resemble the calm before the storm. 'Did she leave because you attacked her?'

There was no anger in me now, only amusement. Understanding this was just more of her mind games, I rested my hand on her desk.

'Did one of my former Met colleagues tell you all this?'

'Possibly.'

I could guess how much fun they'd had on the other end of that phone call.

'Are you so short-staffed you have to play the roles of both the good cop and the bad one?'

She ignored my question, stood and waved to Officer Jules. When she came over, they whispered in each other's ear for two minutes before DI Rose left without a goodbye. I guessed she was more tired than I was. Either that or she'd got what she wanted from that little back and forth.

Jules stared at me with daggers in her eyes – sharp enough to rip out my throat.

'I've been told to take you home. So follow me.'

There was no pretence of formality there.

As we left, a distressed woman entered the building, clutching at her neck and whispering something in Arabic. As an officer took her inside, the woman turned to me.

'They stole my child.'

Before I could reply, she'd scampered through the station, pleading to the officer in a language he obviously couldn't understand.

I followed Jules out and into the police car, taking a short journey back that seemed like an eternity. We didn't speak until I got out of the vehicle.

'Think about moving somewhere else, Walker. The people here don't like coppers, even former ones. And once they find out what you did tonight, your life won't be worth living.'

I stepped towards the car. 'I didn't know you cared, Jules.'

The glare in her eyes told me if she could have beaten me around the head and got away with it, she would have. But instead, she had one last thing to say before leaving.

'You're putting your old man in danger, Walker. You think about that.'

I did that as she drove away, staring at the house next door and wondering how I'd question Dolores without making my situation even worse than it already was.

8 FATHER AND SON

The old man must have gone to bed. He'd left the TV on with the sound muted, so I switched it off and went to my bedroom. The place was cold, a chilled wind invading the landing through an open window in the bathroom. I closed it and took a piss. A sudden weariness seeped out of me, ran down my neck and infested my legs and arms. The time on my watch claimed to be five in the morning, though my body clock screamed, it was close to midnight.

My father had an appointment at the doctor's for ten and, since he refused to take a taxi, it would be a thirty-minute walk. So, if I was lucky enough to hit the hay straight away, I might get three hours of sleep. I wondered if it was worth even getting undressed before crawling under the covers.

I did it anyway, dropping my clothes to the floor and giving the wall one last look before I closed my eyes. I needed to speak to Dolores sooner rather than later, and I had all day to think about how I'd achieve that without ending up in front of Detective Inspector Sara Rose again. I liked the idea of seeing her again, but not if she was arresting me.

———————

SLEEP CAME IN FITFUL BURSTS. Hearing noises from next door, I ignored them when I realised they were only echoes of what had happened. I was up at nine, washed and dressed by ten past. When I got downstairs, my father was sitting in the dining room, a cup of milky tea on the table in front of him. He'd shaved, brushed what little hair he had left into respectable shape, and was wearing a suit.

'Are you going for a job interview?'

His hand shook as he sipped the tea.

'When you get to my age, you always leave the house as if you're heading to your funeral.'

I couldn't tell if he was joking or filled with the morbid realisation he might not make it to the telegram celebrating his hundredth birthday.

I took a glass of water and swilled the last of the toothpaste out of my mouth.

'I think you're only doing it to flirt with the nurses when you get there.'

He laughed through crooked teeth, spilling tea on the table but missing his clean clothes. I wondered how long they'd sat in mothballs. They didn't smell too good.

'Have you seen the nurses there? They all look like Hattie Jacques on a bad day.'

I ignored his attempt at humour. 'Are you sure you don't want to get a taxi? It might be cold out.'

It was the middle of summer and I expected him to boil going up there in that suit.

He got to his feet, his arm wavering as he lifted a trembling finger to point behind me.

'My walking stick is all I need. And do you think we're made of money, wasting it on taxis?' He peered at me as if he was the Grim Reaper and I was his next client. 'You can't have much savings left, can you?'

He'd never complained when I'd returned from London, even though we'd had no contact since a Christmas phone call five years ago. It was soon after Alisha had gone to her family in Delhi and settled the divorce. I wasn't sure why I'd rung him, but the conversation was brief and meaningless.

Then I turned up on his doorstep unannounced a month ago, with all my worldly possessions in one bag. He didn't even speak when he opened the door, just left it open and returned to his chair in the living room. I went inside and spent fifteen minutes explaining why I needed somewhere to stay for a while. I didn't tell him the whole truth: why I'd quit the force or that I had no idea how long I'd be back.

'Your old room is just as you left it,' he'd said.

Then he took twenty pounds out of his shabby trousers and told me to get us both fish and chips. I hadn't explained my financial situation to him, but he must have known how dire it was. Now he was peering at me as if I'd stolen from the police pension fund.

'I've got plenty in the bank,' I said.

I gathered his walking stick and gave it to him. He was still wearing slippers. They were fluffy and had the face of Chewbacca from the *Star Wars* movies covering his toes. I smiled and wondered where he'd got them from.

'You'll need some proper shoes before we go.'

'They're outside in the passage, under the stairs.' It was

a command for me to get them, so I did. 'Take them to the living room and I'll put them on.'

I went in before him, listening to the shuffle of his slippers and his laboured breathing. As far as I knew, he'd never smoked in his life, but now his lungs sounded as if he'd done forty a day for seventy years.

I waited for him to come into the room, contemplating whether I should mention what had happened last night. But he beat me to it as he stepped through the door.

'Why did the police take you away?' He answered the question before I could. 'It was something to do with the Cooks, wasn't it?'

The shoes were in my hand as I bent my knees, removed his slippers and replaced them with footwear designed for walking outside. His feet were tiny, and I saw his toenails about to burst out of his socks. I needed to arrange a visit to the podiatrist for him.

As I helped him, his questions lingered in my mind, their relevance and the importance of what happened with Dolores fading into the background as this moment became something much more significant than putting on a pair of shoes. It was role reversal again, bringing us closer than we had been for years, maybe than we'd ever been.

'How long have you known the neighbours, Dad?'

I shocked myself using that term, and I saw it had the same effect on him.

He struggled for the words, his lips shivering as he spoke.

'Since they moved in, about ten years ago.'

'Have you heard loud noises coming from their house?'

I stood and checked the time on my watch. We'd have to leave soon.

'What type of noises?'

'Oh, you know, shouting and arguing.'

He gripped the stick and limped towards me.

'There are all sorts that go on in this street, Frank. You'll be surprised by what people get up to when they think you're not looking.'

With that enigmatic reply, he was at the front door waiting for me. I locked the door behind us and abandoned the subject for now. As well as focusing on getting him to the doctor's in one piece, I didn't want any accidents and him falling over. I needed to plan a strategy to see Dolores in secret.

For a second, as we moved slowly through the community, I considered holding his free arm like a chaperone, but thought better of it; our burgeoning relationship hadn't developed that far yet. As we walked, I examined the sights of my former childhood: to the right was my primary school, the place where I'd learnt to read and tie my shoelaces, where I met my first girlfriend and had my first kiss. It was also where I'd fallen over and got a face full of dog shit as the other kids howled at me. Even then, I was the tallest kid there, so all it took to get their respect back was for me to crack a few heads.

And I cracked more than a few.

To our left was a row of shops. They were all boarded-up, eaten away by austerity, a failing economy, and online shopping. Plus, all the large retailers had swallowed the smaller places like sharks nibbling on guppies.

We continued, past the houses, including where I was born and lived until I was two. I had no memory of my time there. I observed him as we went, making sure he wouldn't fall and was breathing okay. It was difficult to watch him struggling in the twilight days of his life, and I questioned if I'd done the right thing coming back.

If I hadn't quit my job, would I have returned here? Would I have seen him again before the inevitable?

Fifteen minutes passed, and the swimming baths and medical centre were not far ahead. As I guided him across the road and by the disused pub, a group of teenagers approached on skateboards, giggling and smelling of smoke as they glided past. My lungs yearned for a cigarette as my father paused for breath.

He glared at the kids. 'Why aren't they in school? You never missed any school.'

It was my turn to stare at him, open-mouthed. Attending the primary school we'd just walked by was a happy experience, but that all changed when I went to secondary school; only I didn't really go to it, truanting for most of my last two years. Nicking-off was the term we'd used as kids, and neither the school authorities nor my parents were too concerned about my lack of attendance.

Now, the old man was claiming I'd been a perfect pupil when the truth was the exact opposite for my last two years. When I should have been studying French, maths, English and science, I was sneaking into the cinema, lounging around the parks, or skulking near the shops; not unlike the kids we'd just seen, only they were hardly hiding their light under a bushel.

I was about to tell him of the time I hitchhiked to Manchester to get into the Hacienda to see the Happy Mondays play a benefit gig for the Hillsborough Disaster Appeal, but I thought better of it. It was, ironically enough, on a Monday night, six days after my birthday. I'd told my parents I was staying with a friend over the weekend and would be back on Tuesday. I'd expected them to protest, but they didn't care, and that was fine by me.

'School has changed since you were there, Dad.'

There, I used that word again. I encouraged him to keep moving by glancing at my watch.

'The teachers would whack you over the head if they caught you out of school.' He mentioned it as if it was a bygone day. 'And if a policeman saw you when you should have been there, he'd frogmarch you down to the station to put the fear of God into you. And it worked.'

He spoke with such ferocity, I wondered if what he said might have happened to him. He'd left school at fourteen, whereas I avoided it at the same age. We continued for the medical centre, moving past a Food Bank asking for donations. My father stumbled towards it, reached into his pocket, and handed a woman with a collection tin two ten pound notes. I wasn't sure if it was money he could afford to give away like that. He had a small works pension and an even thinner state one, but I admired him for doing it.

We crossed the road together. As he entered the building, I turned to stare at the woman he'd given the cash to. Once again, I was surprised at how a man of unflinching non-emotion was now discovering what a bit of respect and kindness could do.

Or perhaps I'd been wrong about him all this time, and my memories were false and confused.

Maybe I'd been wrong about many things all this time.

9 DOWN AT THE DOCTORS

It was standing room only in reception. A kind young girl gave up her seat so the old man could sit at the front. I left him there while I spoke to the woman at the desk.

'Hi there.' She acknowledged me without smiling. 'I've brought my father in for some blood tests.' She gazed into her screen and grunted. I took that as an admission she knew we were there. I gave her my best smile; unfortunately, it had failed to woo or impress anyone for some time. 'Is it possible for me to get a wheelchair for him from the NHS? He's finding it difficult to walk.'

She peered over my shoulder at the queue building up behind me.

'You need a referral to the local wheelchair service for an assessment. You'll have to do this before you can get an NHS wheelchair.'

'Can you do it for me?'

If she'd shaken her head any more, I feared it would topple off.

'No. Only his doctor can do that. I'm not important enough.'

She might not have been, but she was an expert on grumpiness. I stepped away and returned to the old man, finding him waxing lyrical with what appeared to be an even older bloke next to him. I left them to it and stood at the side. We were fifteen minutes from his allotted appointment, but there was no guarantee we'd get that on time.

Patients shuffled in and out at a steady pace, the big screen hanging on the wall illuminating when each doctor or nurse was ready to see somebody. I scanned the multitude, observing that all life was there, from expectant mothers to people my father's age who knew the mystery of what comes next was fast approaching.

A man in his forties with a puffed-up red face and milky eyes borrowed from a cow sidled up to me.

'I've got a wheelchair you can have. Is it for your dad?'

The whiteness in his eyes couldn't have been healthy, so at least he was in the right place.

'Yes. He's finding it difficult to walk.'

He'd done well to get to the doctor's, but the wheezing had only increased with every step he'd taken.

'I only live across the road. I'll get it for you.'

He was gone before I could reply, the door sliding shut as I glanced at the patient screen. A message flashed up saying missed GP appointments had cost the NHS £216m last year, with around one in twenty wasted because patients failed to attend without informing the surgery. I was trying to figure out how that calculation worked when my father's name appeared in red neon.

I took him to see the nurse; no need for a doctor since it was only blood tests. After I'd sat him in the corner like a naughty child, I leant towards the friendly-looking woman in the light-blue uniform.

'Excuse me, but do you have the results from his previous tests?'

I kept my voice low in order not to upset him if it wasn't good news, but she had no intention of whispering.

'Are you related to Mr Walker?'

'I'm his son.'

She scrutinised my face, perhaps struggling to see any resemblance to the ageing specimen waiting for her. Or maybe she thought I was lying, that I was some strange oddball who snatched old people off the streets and wheeled them in to see doctors and nurses because of some peculiar fetish.

'Okay. You'll get the full set of results when these have been completed.'

With that, her interest in me was done. She went to him, rolled up his sleeve and exposed an arm not much thicker than my two largest fingers stuck together. His skin was like parchment hanging off him, dotted with bruises where I guessed he'd bumped into something. She glanced at me again as she got a needle, probably thinking I was abusing this poor man now in her care.

'Will it hurt?' he asked her.

'You won't feel a thing, Mr Walker.'

I assumed she was lying by the look on his face as she stuck it in and struggled to suck out enough blood. I waited for his body to shrink like a deflated balloon and melt over the floor, resembling the Wicked Witch of the West. But he pushed out his lips and I watched them quiver. She completed everything in fewer than five minutes, and then we were back in reception. The man with the wheelchair was waiting for us.

'It's got a seat belt and the brakes work.'

For one second, I thought he'd hand me a set of keys.

'Thanks a lot. What do we owe you?'

I reached into my pocket even though there wasn't much there.

He pushed out his lips and shook his head.

'Nothing, mate. The chair was my wife's, but she passed away last month. She'd want someone else to get good use out of it.'

He stuck out his hand, and I took it. 'You're too kind, far too kind.'

The man let go and exited the building as I turned to my father.

He rubbed at his arm. 'I'm not getting in that.'

'I'll push you to the pub if you do.'

It didn't take long for the bribery to kick in.

'No need for that, Frank.' Was that the first time he'd used my name since I'd returned? 'Get me four cans of cider from the shop.'

I pushed him there, bought six cans for us to share, and got the usual fish and chips. At this rate, I'd be rolling back to the doctor's to get fixed for being overweight or diabetic. We ate and drank while watching TV, starting with a game show marathon and finishing with a Jimmy Cagney movie. I emptied the rubbish and cleaned up. By then, it was eight o'clock.

When I returned to the living room, he had a surprise for me. I pointed to his outstretched hand and the key resting inside his wrinkled flesh.

'What's that?'

The liquid in his eyes glistened.

'I know what happened last night with you and the neighbours.'

There was something in his face I don't think I'd ever seen before: concern for me.

'You remember the police being here?'

He rolled his eyes and it was pretty distracting.

'Of course I do. I'm old, not stupid. But they didn't tell me anything.'

'So, how do you know what happened?'

'It's all over the estate. The bloke sitting next to me at the doctor's couldn't wait to tell me. You've given them another reason to hate you.'

'Because they think I attacked Dolores?'

'And that useless husband of hers.' Light flickered through the window and bounced off the key. 'But don't worry, son. I know you better than that.'

I struggled to contain my laughter, lifting my hand to my mouth and nipping at the skin. Here was a man who, as far as I was concerned, had taken no interest in me for the first twenty years of my life and was a stranger after that. Even this last month of us living under the same roof had hardly been a barrel of family laughs.

Then I remembered finding him sitting on the floor with those photographs and recalled the sparkle they had put into him. Of course, they say leopards don't change their spots, but maybe he'd encountered some epiphany in the last twenty-four hours.

I stared again at what was in his hand. Was it a key to some secret family treasure that would rescue both of us from our current torpor?

'Is that for me?'

He nodded. 'It's a spare for next door, for the back. They have one for here, and I have this.'

'What do you want me to do with it?'

'Speak to Dolores. Find out why she lied to the police.

George will be out working until the early hours of the morning.'

'I don't think that's such a good idea, Dad.' There was that word again.

'What else are you going to do? Just sit and take it?'

It wasn't a good idea to go next door, but I'd been thinking about it for much of the day. So what else could I do?

I took the key from him.

'The police could lock me up for this.' Did I care about that? He didn't appear too concerned. Perhaps this was his way of getting rid of me, getting me out of the house so he had it all to himself. 'And the locals won't like it if they find out.'

He shrugged and mouthed those words again.

What else are you going to do?

I left from the back of our house. Now I was calling it our house. It wasn't only the old man who was changing. I climbed over the fence and into the garden. Somewhere in the distance, dogs barked at the gloom descending over the moon. Lights flickered in the house on the other side and I froze. The light illuminated me in the middle of the grass like an incompetent burglar.

The back door opened and a woman stepped out. An open pizza box in her hands obscured her face and my presence. However, it wouldn't be for long once she put that lid down. The key was digging into my palm and I had a split second to drop to the ground, deciding against it since there wasn't enough grass to cover my bulk.

A ten-second wait seemed like an eternity as she closed the lid. I nearly burst out laughing at seeing she was wearing dark glasses. She dropped the empty pizza box and returned inside. I moved before anybody else tumbled into the night, stepping forward and pressing the key into the lock. I turned it and pulled down the handle as quietly as I could. Then I was inside and shutting the door behind me.

There was only one set of lights on, and they came from the living room. I strode towards them and followed the smell of smoke. The fumes clutched at my heart as I moved across the carpet and into the room. Dolores was sitting in a chair in the corner, staring straight at me.

'I've been waiting for you, Frank. Do you want a ciggie?'

More than anything in the world did I want a cigarette.

'Where's George?'

She spat smoke towards me, pointing to a table close to the window with a small card on it.

'He's out in his taxi, getting up to God knows what. His number is on that card. So you can call and talk to him.'

I moved further inside. 'I need some answers from you first. Why did you set me up?'

She dropped the cigarette to the floor, seemingly oblivious to its embers burning into the carpet. That spot must have been damp because it shone like a phoenix before blinking out.

'It wasn't my fault, Frank. Believe me. It was all George's doing; he said it was the only way to pay our debts off.'

'Pay off your debts to whom?'

Dolores lit another cigarette. 'You have to understand that criminals run this town, and gambling is one of their biggest money-makers.'

'Gambling is one of the country's biggest money-makers.'

'It's different here. Once you're in the abyss, it's difficult getting out.'

'So, you sold me out to get clear?'

She nodded through the smoke, her head making a curious bobbing motion like something lost at sea.

'George organised everything. All I had to do was win your confidence.'

And that wasn't hard since she'd found me at my weakest.

'Who were you working for?'

Who in this town hated me that much?

'I don't know. I never saw them. George met them in the pub next door and got all the details there.'

'The pub next door?'

'The Slaughtered Lamb.'

It was called The House when I was a kid, but it appeared as if the new owners had a horror fetish. I turned from her and picked up the card, the smell of smoke drifting over me. I left without giving her another look, going out through the back again. I climbed over the fence and into our garden.

I looked up at the building, peering at the old man's bedroom window before heading through the gap separating our house from the other neighbours.

Now, all I had to do was speak to George Cook and find out who had set me up.

10 TAXI DRIVER

The journey out of the estate took fifteen minutes. Then I crossed from Parish Hills into Bridge End, the streetlights flickering like a scene from a horror movie. When I was a kid, moving out of the Hills and into the End was asking for trouble. Unless you had someone to provide safe passage, you'd get a beating. I didn't know what it was like for adults, but kids needed to be prepared. Luckily, my height and physique had made me immune from such dangers.

It was another ten minutes before I got near the town's oldest green space: Echo Park. When I was ten, I'd climbed a tree in there, suffering from a sudden injection of vertigo, refusing to come down until my mother told the park warden to call the fire brigade to rescue me. I still could remember how embarrassing it was.

I focused on George Cook's phone number and how I'd force the truth from him. Rows of houses stood on either side of me, buildings built just after World War II. Bridge End, like the Hills, was one of those estates the new Labour government constructed after the war to provide cheap rented accommodation for the working classes.

Now, even though the houses were the same, there was minimal rented accommodation left, and what there was had been stripped from the council and handed over to private companies. I had nothing against the government promoting Right To Buy schemes for those renting from their local councils, but the properties sold off were never replaced. So it was near impossible for those at the bottom of the property ladder or people with little money to find affordable places to rent.

These houses were still the same, even if some of them had been tarted up with new brickwork, extensions, or ghastly garden ornaments. To me, they were concrete ghosts, reminders of times I wanted to forget, of wandering through these streets to get away from home or school.

A few residents wandered around, but nobody approached me or spoke. It wasn't long before I was outside the gates with the phone and George's number in my hands.

The park had closed, with a few stragglers or wasters lurking in the trees. Near to me was where they kept the animals: goats and donkeys, llamas and exotic birds imprisoned for the gratification of the people. It was twenty-five years since I'd been there, and I wondered how many creatures had died and been replaced with new ones in that time.

I suppose it doesn't differ from the lives we humans lead, replacing school friends when we drift apart, flitting between work colleagues when we change jobs, even replacing romantic and sexual partners. I had no friends, no job, and no wife anymore, and sexual partners were in the dim and distant past.

But I had the old man.

Is it only families we don't replace? I'd returned to my father to find a different man to the one I'd left all those years ago. However, he'd abandoned me long before that.

A crop of disappointments sprang from the corners of my mind as I peered into the trees. I could go inside, forget about George Cook, see if the tree I was stranded in all those years ago was still there. Then I'd climb it and relive my past, change the stasis in my head by climbing down unaided. I wouldn't need rescuing anymore. There would be no more embarrassment.

Back then, I'd been a fitful boy full of dreams and hopes, yet where was I now but sinking into nightmares I'd hoped were long forgotten? So I dialled Cook's number and waited.

He answered immediately.

'Cook's Cabs, how can I help?'

I lowered my voice, gave him a fake name and told him where to meet me.

As I waited, I zipped up my top and pulled the hood over my head to obscure my face. What would I do if I couldn't get what I wanted from Cook? What would I do to him? Moonlight cut across my vision as calmness settled into my bones. I'd returned home with no precise aim of what to do with my life, just a man running away from circumstances he'd lost control of. Now I had something to pursue, something to reach for.

As the taxi pulled up, I knew what I'd do.

He wound down his window. 'Are you Farmer?' I nodded and climbed into the back of the car. 'You're going to the train station?'

I placed my hand on his shoulder and squeezed.

'There's been a change of plan, George. Drive into the park entrance and turn your lights off.'

Before he refused, I pressed again, only harder this time. His reflection grimaced in the mirror, the pain in his face turning into visible cracks. As he drove the short distance, I eased off when he parked near the locked gates. Then he turned off the engine and I let go.

'I haven't got much money, but take what you want.' Weariness seeped out of him as if this was a regular occurrence in his job.

I pulled my hood down, got out the back, and climbed into the passenger seat.

'Don't worry, George; you'll still get a tip. It might even keep you alive.'

The fear wasn't in his eyes yet, only a residual flicker of defiance.

'The pigs will have you for this, Walker.'

My head was close to his. 'Don't be daft, Georgie boy; even when we're retired, we coppers always stick together. Didn't you know that?'

Somewhere ahead of us, in the park, the sheep started bleating.

'I can't tell you anything.'

His lips quivered as he lied.

'I spoke to Dolores tonight.' I watched that information sink into his thick skull. 'She broke down into a flood of tears, said she still loved you.' I could lie with the best, or worst, of them. 'Dolores told me you were forced into this because of your worsening situation.' I flicked over into good cop mode. 'If you explain it to me, I promise I'll try to help both of you.'

His knuckles whitened as he grabbed the steering wheel.

'We've tried so hard to work for each other, but life doesn't look kindly on people like us.'

I'd heard plenty of sob stories in my time, but he seemed genuine.

'Tell me what happened.'

'Dolores was working in a shop, and I've been trying to make this work.' He removed his fingers from the wheel and pointed at the top of the car. 'But she was on a zero-hours contract, so she was never guaranteed regular hours. This had the knock-on effect of us struggling to get a mortgage or a legal loan. And they didn't have to fire her to get rid of her; all they had to do was stop offering her shifts, and she couldn't do anything about it.' He lifted his head as if urging a greater power to listen to him. 'Everyone is screwing you over, especially the bosses.'

'So, you became your own boss?'

George let out a high-pitched screech of a laugh.

'I tried, but it didn't work. I couldn't afford the extra insurance on the car and the cost of repairs. So I took a position with a local firm, but I'm not classed as a permanent worker.'

'You only get paid for the jobs or gigs you do?'

'Yeah, but now, it isn't many.'

'Which meant you couldn't pay your bills. So you fell into debt and tried to gamble your way out of it, which led to even more debt. Is that right?'

His answer was to place his head on the steering wheel.

'Then I got offered a grand to stitch you up.'

When he lifted his face, an imprint of the car's logo was on his forehead.

'Who gave you the money?'

'I don't know, Walker; I swear to God. I was drowning my sorrows in the Slaughtered Lamb last week, sulking in the corner because I could only afford half a pint when he sidled up to me. He never gave me his name, but I can tell you what he looked like.'

'Go on.'

He scrambled through his memory.

'About six feet tall, medium build, blue eyes, with a mass of red curly hair. You won't mistake this guy if you see him.'

'You'd never seen him before that night?'

'No.'

I gazed into his face and believed him. 'Take me home, George.'

He relaxed and drove away. After that, he was silent until we got there.

'What now, Walker?'

I stepped out of the car and handed him a fiver.

'You go to the police and ask for DI Rose. Then you tell her exactly what you told me tonight. You got that?'

He nodded and I went inside. It was late and I guessed the old man would be in bed, but he wasn't. Instead, he was sitting in the usual chair as I entered the living room. He switched off the TV.

'How did it go?'

I told him about the conversations I'd had with Dolores and George. Then I placed the key on the arm of the sofa.

'When George tells the police the truth, and they confirm it with Dolores, I can leave it with them. Then, they'll search for this redheaded man. Have you ever seen a bloke like that, around here or in the pub?'

He shook his head. 'I haven't been in there for years.'

I slumped into the sofa opposite him.

'When I was a kid, you were in that pub every day.'

'I had a falling out with the landlord a few years back, but it's changed owners now.'

'So, why don't you go back in?'

He shrugged. 'You should never go back, Frank.'

With those words, he went to bed. My mind continued to be a ball of confusion and I wasn't ready for sleep. So I sat up for another few hours and pondered my options before deciding on one.

It was time to get the old man back into the Slaughtered Lamb. Only this time, I'd be with him, and we wouldn't be leaving until I found out who was out to get me.

11 HAPPY HOUR

It was gone eleven when I made it downstairs the next morning. The old man was in his usual spot, wearing his suit again.

I scratched my chin. 'Are you going somewhere?'

'Your mother told me we have to go shopping. There's no food in the house.'

The itch raced to the front of my head. My mother hadn't been in this house for twenty years. She lived in a care home ten miles away, if you could class it as living. There was nothing and nobody she recognised anymore. The last time I'd visited, she'd stared right through me as if I was invisible. It wasn't much different from how she'd looked at me during my childhood, but the vacancy behind her eyes in that place shook me to the core. I couldn't face going back there.

I went and peered out the window. The itch continued, so I tried to ignore it. It was sunny outside, so why not go out? We could test the wheelchair again.

'I've got a better idea, Dad.' It shocked me how easily

the word fell from my tongue. 'I'll push you to the park. We'll eat in the café there and look at the animals.'

He pondered my question before nodding. 'Can I get a bacon sandwich?'

'You can have whatever you want.'

I sat down and put my shoes on, then got a scarf for him. Getting him into the wheelchair was easier than I expected; not the physical mechanics, but how he accepted the idea with no moaning or whinging.

We travelled the same route I'd done last night for my meeting with George Cook, but this took a lot longer. The sun beat down on my face, and I was sweating within the first ten minutes. At least two buses went past as I struggled up the road. The old man weighed little, so this must have been down to how unfit I was. I needed to get back to the gym as soon as possible; once I found the redheaded bloke and cleared my name.

'It'll be easier coming back, Frank; it's all downhill.'

I didn't tell him it would be easier because we'd be getting a taxi. I still had George's number, so perhaps I'd call him.

There was no other conversation between us until we got to the park. I was too tired to speak, and it was never his thing, anyway. As I pushed him through the main gate, a group of kids raced towards a noticeboard. There was a list of events and times on it. I checked to make sure the café was open, desperate for a cold drink. There were posters on the board about missing dogs and one looking for information about a sixteen-year-old boy who was last seen in the park six weeks ago.

'We'll get some food first, Dad.'

I pushed him past the not so exotic animals, my legs throbbing as we weaved our way to the café. We spent an hour there, giving me time to recover and having a large breakfast each. We took a slow journey back through the enclosures, but I could see he was both sleepy and bored. The taxi was waiting for us as we got to the gates, but it wasn't George. I'd thought better of speaking to him again so soon and called another company instead. George could sweat a little before our next meeting, the outcome of which would depend upon me getting information about the redheaded bloke.

The afternoon had tired the old man out when we returned home, so he was snoring in his chair five minutes after slumping into it. I went to my room, got out my phone, and trawled the internet until it turned dark outside.

We were out again, dead on seven. Since the pub was three hundred yards from us, Jack refused to be guided into the wheelchair, no matter how hard I tried to convince him.

'All I need is my walking stick and your arm.'

I escorted him on my search for the redheaded man, gathering firm looks and stern silence as we entered the Slaughtered Lamb. It was an eerie quiet reminiscent of how the air sounds before a bomb drops. Then the customers and woman behind the bar returned to their business, and I ushered him into a seat near the door.

'I'll get you a cider.'

I scanned the pub as I went to the bar. I'd been in here a few times as a kid, sent by my mother to bring him home before the food got cold. It was under a different name then, but the decor had hardly changed in three decades. The carpet was worn and beer stained, the walls dotted with old photos of the building and the local football team, while an occasional flashing machine illuminated the gloom. It was one of those places that did without a jukebox, and for once, I was glad. I needed to hear myself think.

As for the people, I knew none of them, but recognised the types. There were four young lads, possibly late teens, early twenties, playing pool in the corner. They were clad in designer sports clothes as if preparing for an Olympic event. Opposite where I'd plonked the old man was a group of pensioners, maybe twenty years younger than him, shuffling dominoes. Five-and ten-pound notes fluttered in the middle of the table, and it appeared to be a much more serious game than I'd ever played.

Further into the bar were half a dozen thirty-something women carrying giant inflatable penises and downing copious amounts of fizz. I avoided their gaze and ordered two pints of cider from the server. She was half my age and gave me a warm smile. I told her to keep the change when she delivered the drinks.

'I'm Grace,' she said as I thanked her. I was about to give her my name when she stopped me with a carefully placed touch on my wrist. 'Everyone around here knows who you are, Frank.'

'My reputation precedes me.'

She laughed and removed her hand. 'Something like that.'

I used this as my first opportunity to get some information. If anybody knew about the pub's customers, it would be her.

'I'm trying to find an old friend of mine, Grace. He was in here last week, a tall bloke, smaller than me, with a shock of curly red hair. Have you seen him?'

The warmth in her face vanished, replaced with a cold, hard stare.

'I don't know anyone like that. What's his name?'

That was a great question, one I should have been asking her.

'Everyone just calls him Curly.'

'I'm sorry, I've never seen him in here.'

She turned from me to serve another punter, and I took the drinks back to our seats. The old man grabbed his and grinned at me.

'She's far too young for you, son.'

He wasn't wrong. I had a large gulp of cider and enjoyed the sickly sweetness washing down my throat. Who else was there to ask in this motley collection of people? Before I could decide, one of them spoke to me.

'You're not welcome here, copper. This place is only for locals.'

A pool-playing Olympian had detached himself from his group and loomed over our table. He was tall, maybe a few inches shorter than me, and built like a rugby player. He was holding a pool cue, his knuckles throbbing ruby red with the pressure he was applying to the wood.

I took another sip and licked my lips.

'Kid, I was inside this place long before you were born, and he,' I tilted my head towards my father, 'fought the fascists so people like you could dress as idiots and pretend you were tough guys. And I'm not a copper.'

Everywhere was silent as I finished. His mates looked over in anticipation; the domino gamblers had laid down their pieces and gazed at me, while the gaggle of women dropped their giant plastic dicks and spilt Prosecco over the floor. Then the kid lifted the pool cue and slammed it into the carpet.

'Leave, or I'm going to smash this over your head.'

I let out a long sigh and pushed my pint glass to one side. I'd hoped to talk my way out of this pointless pissing contest, but it seemed unlikely now. I stood and faced him, my eyes burning into his. His friends weren't moving, so perhaps I could get it over and done with no other interference. The key was to get him to make the first move.

'What's your problem, kid? I only want to sit here with my father and have a quiet drink.'

He snarled at me. 'I don't care what you want. Coppers and their families aren't wanted here.' He glanced around the room for apparent encouragement. 'We all know what you did to George and Dolores.'

That was annoying, the fact Cook hadn't told the police the truth yet, which meant no one in this insular community knew either.

'I never touched Dolores. She and George will confirm that if you ask them.'

He took a step back, and I guessed he was preparing to attack me with that cue. The table was between him and me, leaving little room for manoeuvre. I grabbed my pint as the old man sipped at his. Before I could move away from him, the pool man's arm was in the air, ready to whack me round the head with that long, thin slice of wood. So I kicked the table into his legs, hearing it crack against his knees. He dropped the cue to the floor and clasped at his damaged bones. Then he looked up at me with pure hate in his eyes.

'I'm going to kill you for that.'

He pounced at me – the folly of youth – with hands outstretched and reaching for my throat. I caught his right wrist and twisted it, the bone snapping with a fearsome crack. His scream rattled the dominoes on the table. I kept holding his hand and pushed him back until he collapsed into the quiz machine near him. A glance over my shoulder told me his friends weren't interested in getting involved. The pint was in my other hand, and I drank from it while the old man raised his to me.

I increased the pressure on the wrist and leant into his flushed face.

'You can leave now or stay. It's up to you.'

Behind his eyes was a burning desire to thrash out, scream and shout, but somewhere in the dark corners of his brain, a fraction of reason must have existed since he nodded to me. I let go of him and stepped back. I picked up the pool cue as he staggered to his feet. I offered it to him, but he refused, stumbling past me and out of the pub. His friends followed with tails between their legs. I returned the table to its original spot and finished the rest of my drink.

The old man grinned at me. 'Just like the good old days.'

I went to the bar for another cider. The women on the hen night had gone, leaving a deflated plastic penis draped over the back of a chair. I ordered a pint from Grace. She spoke to me as she pulled it.

'You shouldn't have done that, Frank.'

'I had no choice.'

She shook her head, a grim countenance covering her face.

'That kid was Phil Thompson.'

She handed the glass to me, and I paid.

'Am I supposed to know who that is?'

'His father is Tony Thompson. He runs this estate. You get on the wrong side of him and you're in for it.'

I sipped at the cider. 'I was at school with a Tony Thompson. Is it the same one?'

Fear gripped her eyes. 'I don't know. I think he's about your age, so maybe it's him. You should drink up and go.'

I smiled at her and glanced at my father. At least he was still awake.

'He's enjoying himself too much for us to leave.'

I winked at her, finding myself flirting against my better

judgement. Taking my pint back to the table, I placed it down and turned to the domino crew.

They stared at me in unison. 'What do you want, Walker?'

'Just some information, fellas.' I squeezed into the only available spot without an invitation. 'I'm looking for a man with distinctive curly red hair. Do any of you know who or where he is?'

The bloke next to me scowled at his dominoes, a double six in his hand and nowhere to put it. He slammed it face down and turned to me.

'Even if we knew him, why would we tell you?'

'Maybe because you're all upstanding citizens of society?'

They laughed together, a raucous cackle reminiscent of a pack of hyenas howling at the moon. Then, when they'd stopped and wiped the spit from their chins, the double-six-man spoke again.

'There's no such thing as society, Walker. Didn't your old man ever tell you that?'

The doors opened before I could reply and two goons strode in as if they owned the place. My new domino-playing friends rose as one, a lot quicker than I would have believed they could at their age. They scrambled up the money and left through the exit at the opposite end of the pub. I returned to my seat as the goons headed to the bar.

My father still had half a pint to drink. 'Now it's going to get interesting.'

The bigger of the men pressed a phone to his chewed-up ear, and then nodded as if whoever was on the other end could see him.

I leant into the old man. 'Do you know who they are?'

'You'll soon find out, son.'

He wasn't wrong. Two more goons came through the door, followed by a purple-faced Phil Thompson. The smartly dressed bloke behind him could only have been his father. They shared the same rugged gammon features: all piggy eyed and pockmarked cheeks as if some distracted Creator had given up on them halfway through. Tony Thompson listened to something his son whispered before walking over to me.

The last time I'd set eyes on him, he was face down in a ditch. Age hadn't improved his appearance. Or the whine of his voice.

'Well, well, Frank Walker, as I live and breathe.' He pulled a chair opposite me and sank into it. 'It's time to settle some old scores, don't you think?'

12 POLICE AND THIEVES

Two of Tony's goons stood behind him while the others guarded both doors. Was this to stop people from entering the pub or because they thought I'd try to do a runner and abandon the old man?

Phil Thompson nursed his damaged wrist at the bar.

'You should get your kid to the hospital, Tony, before the bone sets in the wrong place and he ends up even more useless than he is now.'

One of his men placed two glasses of bourbon on the table between us.

'You know, Frank, when people told me you'd returned to live with your old fella, I didn't believe them.' He grabbed his drink and swallowed half of it. 'I thought it couldn't be true that Frank Walker would be stupid enough to come back to where nobody wanted him. So I said it must have been that older brother of yours, the one who joined the army and went missing. What was his name, Tommy?'

'Thomas.' My father spoke as he took the bourbon intended for me and downed it. He glared at Thompson. 'If you're handing out free booze, I'll have another.'

Tony nodded at his goons. Soon, there were three fresh drinks on the table.

I peered at him. 'What do you want, Tony?'

He glanced at his kid. 'You hurt my son, Frank. I can't let that go unpunished, not with my reputation in the community.'

I nearly spat the booze all over him. 'Things must have changed in the twenty-five years I've been away.' I put the glass down. 'Does your gang know what we used to call you at school?'

The redness increased in his cheeks so he resembled a fresh apple.

'Don't make it worse for yourself, Frank.'

'What was it again?' I scratched at my nose in mock forgetfulness. 'That's it, Tony the Toenail. You hated going to gym classes because we all saw how horrible your toenails were. Did you ever get that sorted?'

The blood drained from his face faster than water from a leaky pipe.

'You should let your father go home, Frank. It'll be better for both of you.'

I hoped my smile would dazzle him enough to distract his tiny mind. I had no chance against his four goons. So what was I to do? Distracting him some more seemed to be my best bet. As a teenager, he'd been a vain little twit. Considering the expensive suit and flash jewellery he was wearing, I didn't think he'd changed.

'So, you're the king of the castle on this estate, Tony. How the hell did that happen? You couldn't lead a dog when we were kids, so what miracle kissed you on those ruddy cheeks?'

He shifted in his chair. 'I guess I was always cleverer than you and everyone else thought.' He glanced around the bar at his child and his thugs, ignoring Grace cleaning a glass. 'Give the people what they want, and they'll reward you in many ways.'

'And what do you give the people of Parish Hills?'

He shrugged. 'Every group needs to be led, desires protection and guidance, and they need to feel safe. That's the role I play here and in other estates in the town.'

'You sound like quite a generous guy, Tony, but aren't their other organisations who do those things? The government, the schools, social services and the police?'

Thompson placed his hands on the table, his fingernails perfectly manicured. He smelt of Chanel for Men.

'Living in London must have scrambled your northern genes into mush, Frank. I bet you eat your pizza with a knife and fork, don't you?' His laugh rattled his teeth. 'All those groups you mentioned abandoned the communities here ages ago. Underfunding, cuts and closures left towns like this teetering on the brink of anarchy for a while. Kids don't trust their teachers, and the schools are understaffed and overworked. Social services keep trying to put out fires while the staff are leaving in droves. The government only cares about areas where they can win elections. And as for the police, well,' he scratched one of those perfect nails into the table, 'if they're not fixing people up for crimes, they're abusing those they're supposed to be protecting.'

'Abusing?'

'Don't tell me they're all squeaky clean where you worked, Frank. Around here, we've had a Chief of Police sacked on corruption charges and at least three police officers who had to quit after women and girls accused them of sexual assault. They got off scot-free, of course.'

Everything he said was true, but the glue that held society together would only survive if the bonds of civilisation forged over the years were adhered to. And I knew from bitter experience that crooks like him would always rub at that glue until it disappeared.

'You and others stepped in to look after the people here? At what cost?'

'Capitalism and democracy go hand in hand, Walker. This is the modern world we live in.'

His use of my surname showed that his fake bonhomie was about to disappear soon at my expense.

'You don't like the police coming here?'

The red in his eyes was increasing by the second.

'We deal with our own problems. There're no drugs or druggies in this estate, no petty criminals or muggers. There hasn't been a murder in a dozen years. So we don't need the authorities telling us what justice is. That's the way it's worked for a long time, until you turned up.'

'I never touched Dolores. It was a lie created by her husband after somebody paid him to do it. Someone he met in this pub. If you're the Lord of the Hills, Tony, you should know who this bloke is – six feet tall with striking curly red hair. I think he'd be a hard one to miss, especially with your connections. Do you know his name?'

He grinned and shook his head.

'I'm not here to answer your questions, Walker. And you're not a copper anymore.' He leant so close to me, I could smell the garlic on his breath. 'Is it true you lost your job because you threatened a serial killer? How funny is that?'

He was about to laugh before I moved forward and grabbed his hand. It had worked on his kid, so why not with him?

'If any of your thugs move, Tony, I'll crush your fingers before they reach me. You always fancied yourself as a bit of an Elton John impersonator, but you'll never play the piano again.'

His face contorted until he looked like a fleshy version of Munch's *The Scream*. The two goons behind him were wavering until he spoke through gritted teeth.

'Stay where you are, boys, I'll deal with this.'

I increased the pressure on his fingers.

'Well done, Tony. Perhaps you'll make a decent citizen after all.'

Blood swirled inside his eyes as he puffed out his cheeks.

'You're only making things worse for you and the old man, Walker. You'll have to let go of me, eventually. Then what will you do?'

It was an excellent question. I could make him tell his thugs to leave, but they'd only wait for me outside, in the dark. Then how would I get my father home in one piece?

'Tell me the truth, Tony. Even with that sanctimonious speech you've just given me, you're nothing more than a local gangster, a few levels below the Kray twins, aren't you?'

I released my grip a little to allow him to breathe without snapping his lungs.

'People like me keep the peace as much as possible in this town. You can call me whatever you want, insult me like you did when we were kids, but I'm a saviour to folks like her.' He nodded at Grace. She'd put the glass down to stare at me. 'One word from me and the boys will do to her what you're doing to me. How will that make you feel, Walker?'

I'd feel like shit; that's how I'd feel. I was well on my way to feeling like that already. What was my next move? I considered my options before releasing his hands. His smirk irritated me.

I flexed my fingers in front of his face.

'Do you know how easy it is to scoop out a human eye, Tony?' Fear replaced his stupid grin. 'I could have two digits inside your socket and the eye out after a couple of seconds. I might even get the other one if you don't thrash around before your boys reach me.' I let the information sink through his thick skull for a second. 'Then, do you think people will perceive you as their saviour if you can't see?'

The lines on his face appeared to wobble as he spoke.

'What do you want?'

'I want you to tell Grace to take the rest of the night off, but first, she has to come over here and take my father home. Can you do that for an old friend, Tony?'

I grabbed his hand as if I was about to propose, and he didn't appear excited by the prospect. Then he did as I'd requested. Grace was around the bar and helping the old man out of his seat quicker than an Olympic sprinter.

My father looked pleased. 'I can't remember the last time someone so pretty held my arm,' he said to her.

She got him past the goons and out of the door as Thompson continued to glare at me.

Now how was I going to get out of this conundrum?

I pressed my thumb into his knuckle.

'Tell me who this redheaded man is and I'll let you go.'

'I don't know who you're talking about. I've been abroad for a month and only got back two days ago. So that's why I was shocked to hear you were home again.'

His goons appeared restless, crunching their knuckles and glaring at me.

'If you're the kingpin you claim you are, Tony, then

you'd know everything going on around here. And who else would have a grudge against me if it wasn't you?'

The laughter spurted out of him, spit dripping on my fingers as I gripped his hand.

'You have selective amnesia, don't you, Walker?' He lifted his free hand and wiped it across his mouth. 'You mentioned my nickname, but do you remember what everyone called you? It was appropriate; what with you ending up in the east end of London.'

'I forget, Tony. Was it as good as Toenail?'

He didn't let my jab get to him, seemingly getting used to the pain in his hand. Instead, he turned to his thugs.

'Are any of you guys *EastEnders* fans? Can you guess what we called Frank here?'

His goons glanced at each other in confusion until the most cultured one came up with the answer.

'His nickname was Butcher?'

'Spot on, Lucas. But it wasn't just because there was a character named Frank Butcher on that terrible TV show.' He switched back to me. 'It was because you were a prime thug and bully, weren't you, Frank? That's why you ran off to London, because you'd upset so many in this town. I'm sure there's not only me here who thinks you're due some retribution.'

His grin magnetised me. Had I forgotten that part of my past? I was different when I got to London; I remembered that. I reinvented myself in a fresh environment, with new people, surrounded by bright lights and a thousand opportunities. But had I been the bully he now claimed? I had no memory of those things.

But the name Butcher resonated inside the corners of my mind.

Frank the Butcher.

A song drifted into my mind.

Butcher Baby. Butcher baby, I'm coming for you.

Was this all about someone from my past wanting revenge? All those messages on the doorstep, the plastic pig's head, even this thing with Dolores and George Cook?

'This was twenty-five years ago and more, Tony. You need to forget about it and move on.'

I let go of his hand and sat back in the seat, resigned now to what would come next.

He clenched the fingers I'd released, making a fist as the blood returned to his face.

'The past always catches up with you, Butcher. I thought you coppers knew that.'

Before I could remind him I wasn't in the force anymore, there was a kerfuffle at the door. The goon guarding it stumbled inside and jabbed his side into the bar. Then, to my surprise and, I assumed, everyone else's, DI Rose strode into the pub, followed by two uniformed police officers.

She pointed at me. 'Frank Walker, you're coming with me.'

The tension in the room increased. Thompson may have claimed to be the authority in this community, but I doubted he wanted a confrontation with the police right here, right now. He got up, still flexing his damaged hands.

'You're not needed here, copper. You know we take care of our own.'

She appeared indifferent to his show of bravado.

'Is that so, Thompson? Then maybe you can tell me who killed George Cook.'

The bar went silent.

Inside my head, The Clash were playing *Police and Thieves.*

DI Rose didn't speak again until we were sitting in the police car.

'It looked like you and Thompson were having a nice chat.'

The estate sped by us outside the window.

'Me and Toenail go way back.'

'Toenail?'

'It's a school thing. He claims to be the kingpin in this community, to have more powers than the police. Is that true?'

'I don't know what things are like in the capital, Walker, but in small northern towns, it's a bit more complicated.'

'You let petty criminals do your job for you?'

'There's nothing petty about Thompson and his ilk.'

'He seems to think he controls this community. Does he?'

The car shuddered to a stop at a red light. Her eyes matched the illumination outside.

'I'm the one asking the questions here, Walker, not you.'

I smiled at her. 'Call me Frank. Or Butcher. What happened to George Cook?'

'That's what you're going to tell us at the station.'

That was the end of the conversation until I was back at the cop shop, this time inside an interview room with DI Rose and her colleague, Detective Sergeant Debbie Smith.

At least I wasn't handcuffed.

'Do I need a lawyer?'

DI Rose peered at me. 'Do you want one?'

'Am I being charged with anything?'

'Not yet. But there's still time.'

'What happened to George Cook?' I asked again.

Nobody had read me my rights and there was no recording going on. So I relaxed a little. We classed this as an informal chat back when I was a copper. That thought made it sound so long ago, and not a short hop into my previous life.

'Were you with him last night?'

I didn't see the point in lying. Plus, it was apparent she knew I was.

'I called his taxi and he took me home.'

'Where did he meet you?'

'Outside the gates of Echo Park.'

'When was that?'

'Ten o'clock.'

'How long was the drive from there to your house?'

How strange it was to be on the other side of this technique, observing her trying to pick me apart one small question at a time and root out the truth by a thousand tiny cuts slicing through a cloak of deception. Only I had nothing to hide, and I wasn't one of them anymore.

'Maybe ten minutes.'

She removed a notepad from her jacket and flicked

through the pages. It was weird to see such an archaic method in a modern police station. Even the Beat Bobbies had personal digital devices to record everything in London. There was no need to write anything down when every instance, word or movement could be captured on audio or video. I guessed resources were lacking in the sticks.

'George recorded the pickup outside Echo Park before ten o'clock and the drop off at ten-thirty. So what were you doing for that extra twenty minutes in the car?'

DS Smith grinned at me from behind her superior officer, and I had to control the irritation scratching away at my insides.

'We had a conversation.'

Rose had a pen in her hand, placed on the pad ready to note the words she probably assumed I was about to condemn myself with. But my conscience was clear. I had nothing to fear from the truth.

'What did you talk about?'

'I asked him why he'd lied to the police.'

She didn't write that down. 'What was his reply?'

I told her the tale he'd told me about the redheaded man and the plot to frame me.

'He said he'd tell you this himself, in person, today.'

DI Rose shook her head. 'The first time I saw him today was in the morgue, and he was in no state to talk to anyone.' She placed a hand on her throat. 'Someone strangled him around midnight. He wasn't a pretty sight, lying on that slab.'

I didn't need a description from her. I'd seen the faces of victims of strangulation. It was a terrible way to die. Not that I believed there were any good ways, but at least some had to be more peaceful than others.

'I was at home at midnight.'

'So you say.'

She peered at the notebook again and I wondered if anything was written in it.

'How do you know he picked me up?'

Did I give him a false name when I made the call? I couldn't remember. It wouldn't look good if I did.

'We have an eyewitness.'

'An eyewitness? It was dark and I had a hood over my head.'

'That sounds suspicious, Frank.'

'It was cold. So how could anyone see my face?'

'We have a description of your physique. How many men do you think are in this town with your build? What are you, six foot five and weighing over two hundred pounds? You're a unique specimen.'

'Well, good luck using that in court.'

She smiled at me. 'Who mentioned going to court? As I said earlier, we're not charging you with anything. I only want to be clear on your whereabouts last night.' She flicked through the pages again. 'It appears as if our murderer wore gloves to strangle Mr Cook, but our forensic people told me they're confident of getting DNA evidence from the vehicle.'

'I already said I was in the car, so that means nothing.' I gazed straight into her eyes; the not-yet accused facing down their potential accuser. 'Which is why your eyewitness claim is bullshit. I told you I was in the car with him, and why.'

'How did you get his number?'

My hesitation gave me away. Could I say I found it on the internet? Was he even listed there? Since he was working for himself, I didn't expect him to log his calls anywhere. And what was the name I'd given him? And why was I having problems with my memory?

'Dolores gave it to me.'

This time, DI Rose wrote something in the notebook. She stared at it for a few seconds before looking at me.

'Let me get this straight. Less than a day after we found you inside your neighbour's Dolores and George Cook's home, a house you entered uninvited, and both Mr and Mrs Cook accused you of attacking them, you went back inside to see the wife?' I didn't need to confirm what she said. 'How did you get into the house?'

I could feel those thousand cuts biting into me.

'My father gave me the spare key the neighbours left with him in case of emergencies. They have one for our house.'

'You let yourself into the house, uninvited, once again?' She didn't wait for an answer she could guess I wouldn't give. 'To see a woman who had accused you of not only stalking her, but attacking her as well?'

The way she put it didn't sound good.

'I needed to know why she lied. And she told me the truth.'

'According to you. This would be the redheaded man who gave them a thousand pounds to stitch you up, allegedly.'

'Doesn't that make more sense than me, a short time after I got here, starting an affair with my next-door neighbour's wife, and then beating them both up when she ended it?'

She put down her pen. 'You were a copper for twenty-five years, Frank, and in a much more cosmopolitan environment than this one. Are you saying what you just told me, that those types of human relationships didn't happen all the time there, and you and your colleagues weren't faced with the consequences of those actions?'

I puffed out my cheeks. How could I deny what she said?

'It wasn't how they claimed. Ask Dolores now; she'll tell you the truth.' But would she? I wasn't convinced of it, but with George murdered, there was no one else to verify what I said. 'Just ask Dolores.'

DI Rose picked up the pen and rolled it between her fingers.

'I wish we could speak to Mrs Cook, but we haven't been able to find her since the discovery of her husband's body. When my colleagues forced their way into the house, it looked like a bomb had gone off in there. And there was no sign of Dolores.'

DI Rose moved closer to me. 'Tell me, Frank, if you were in my place, how would you think it looks when we have a murdered husband, missing wife, and only the day before both of them accused their neighbour of attacking them? What would you do?'

What would I do? Exactly what she was doing now. But I wouldn't say that to her.

'I'd search for the man with the shock of curly red hair.'

She slid into the back of her chair, with one hand flung into the air as if she wanted to hit me with a cartoon mallet. She gazed at me for at least a minute before grabbing her notebook and pen.

'Even if your mystery redheaded bloke was still in town, how easy do you think it would be to find someone amongst a population close to a hundred and fifty thousand based on such a limited description?'

'And you with minimal resources.'

She smiled as if it was the first sensible thing I'd said since getting here.

'Exactly.'

'So, you're not arresting me?'

'No, not yet. You'll give DS Smith here a full statement, everything you've told me, and we'll take it from there.'

'That's great.' It wasn't, but it was better than it could have been.

She got up. 'Tell me, Frank, why would this mystery redheaded man go to all this trouble to get to you?'

That was the sixty-four thousand dollar question I didn't have the answer for, but I gave her a reply as she headed for the door.

'When I find out, I'll let you know, DI Rose.'

After she left, DS Smith led me to her desk and typed out my statement. It took more than an hour. And afterwards, there was no lift back.

I walked home, through the dead streets and underneath the flickering lights, my mind consumed with the events of the night. George Cook could only have been murdered by the redheaded man, unless it was a random killing of a taxi driver. It happened in and around London, but it seemed unlikely here. Thompson had told me there hadn't been a murder in the town for over ten years. Now we had one – the guy paid to frame me. And his wife was missing. Why would the killer take her? Perhaps it was another way of getting at me, but for what? I hadn't been here for over two decades, so why now? Thompson claimed people from my past had grudges against me, but he was hardly a bastion of truth.

Then there was Thompson himself. He wouldn't let what happened in the pub go without a response; his ego and so-called reputation couldn't allow it. So perhaps it would be a good idea to move out of the house and not put the old man in danger.

All of those things pounded my head as I walked home. When I arrived, the light was still on in the living room. I went in, finding him asleep in his chair. I left him there, was heading to my bed when he called my name.

'I've got something for you, Frank.'

There was a piece of paper in his outstretched hand. I took it and stared at an address.

'What's this, Dad?'

'It's Grace's address. She wants you to go there after dark tomorrow. Round the back, so no one sees you.'

I wasn't in the mood for flirtation. 'Why would I do that?'

'Because she said she knows who you're searching for.'

'What?'

'The redheaded man. She said his name was Harpo. Grace wouldn't tell me any more. She'll only speak to you face to face.'

I looked at the address again before slipping it into my pocket.

'Do you need a hand upstairs?'

He shook his head, looking all of his ninety-three years.

'No thanks, son. There's a late showing of *The Wild Bunch* on soon. So I'm going to watch that.'

I left him to his western and went to bed, that name ringing in my ears.

Harpo.

Just like the curly-haired Marx Brother.

I lay awake and wondered if my antagonist couldn't talk either.

I intended to spend the rest of the day inside, not showing my face unless any irate locals decided they were brave enough for a confrontation. Grace's address was only a short walk from the pub, around the corner and behind my old primary school. She'd said to go after dark, but I was impatient. If I took a risk, I could sneak across the school's playing field to the back of her house without anyone seeing me.

But my father had other ideas.

'We need to go to the rent office.' He waved a small plastic card at me as I stepped into the living room. 'It was due last week.' Worry seeped out of his eyes. 'I don't want them kicking me out of here. Those Andreas bastards will have you out in a second, and then sell this place to the highest bidder.'

I hadn't seen him this agitated in a while. 'Are you sure they can do that, Dad?'

His fingers shook so much I thought he'd drop the card and fall out of the chair. Instead, I moved closer and took it from his hand. A nineteen-digit number was printed into it, plus his name and the words Andreas Housing. When I'd lived here as a kid, my parents had rented it from the local council. Then, sometime into the new millennium, it was bought by a private company. It appeared to have since been sold again to a different business.

'You don't know what they're like. They've sold many houses on this road to private landlords and pocketed the profits. Do you think they want a man of my age living on his own in a large three-bedroomed house?'

'You've been here for over forty years, Dad; you must have some rights?'

He shook his head, trembling fingers wiping whatever he'd eaten for breakfast from his quivering lips.

'I thought you were cleverer than this, Frank. Help me up and we'll pay it together.'

'Can't it be done online?'

'I don't know what that is. Just let me pay at the office.'

He didn't look capable of going far, even if I pushed him in the wheelchair.

'I'll do it; you stay here and relax.'

It was the least I could do since I'd been staying in the house rent-free for over a month. I'd have to risk the wrath of the locals if it came to it.

He flopped back into his chair without the expected argument.

'Get some food as well. The kitchen's empty again.'

He was right. My usual routine of buying stuff to last me two days would have to change if I intended living here much longer.

Did I want to stay here for another month? Six months? A year? I'd given it no thought when I'd left London, but now I had to consider what my plans were. I wouldn't go while the police searched for a killer and a missing woman.

And I couldn't leave until I found the redheaded man. It appeared as if my choices were being made for me.

'Okay. I'll bring something hot back with me.'

I locked the front door behind me, glancing at the neighbours' house as I left. How serious would this under-staffed and poorly resourced police force treat Dolores Cook's disappearance? The police treat each missing person's case differently, and their response would depend on several factors. First, they'd conduct a risk assessment to decide the correct response to Dolores's case. This reaction would then depend on various aspects, including age, vulnerability, physical or mental health conditions, the time elapsed since last seen, circumstances of disappearance, and whether Dolores had been missing before. George's murder and her report about me would put Dolores at the top of the list.

Unfortunately, it would also place me at the top of another list.

Dolores's face was at the forefront of my mind as I headed for the rent office. Once, the street had been a wide avenue with rows of languid trees on either side. On the right, they'd guarded the primary school where I'd spent five years of my academic life; on the left had been a set of flats for pensioners and a collection of shops. Those homes had been demolished and replaced with gentrified apartments rented out by the same organisation I was on my way to see. The shops of my youth had also disappeared, substituted by bookmakers, a place selling vapes, and a mobile phone emporium.

The trees were also gone, displaced by a mess of dishevelled grass and concrete benches that had seen better days. As a kid, I'd taken this journey to school. Now, the youngsters were ferried there by adults and cars, and you rarely saw them playing on the streets. At least that's what I'd found since my return. The few I'd observed always had their faces buried in digital devices and appeared to be oblivious to the world around them.

The good thing about this was that few people noticed me as I made my way through the estate and entered the Andreas Housing offices. Next to it were the local swimming baths, and I got a blast of chlorine as I went to pay the old man's rent.

It was one of those modern places that could have fitted in somewhere in Dante's seven layers of Hell: soulless, cold, populated with grey furniture and blank walls.

I approached the reception and the man behind the desk. His face was caked in boredom, streaked with tedium and world-weariness. He looked like someone who'd got lost on the way to buy a pint of milk and found himself in the belly of a cow he couldn't escape from. His voice was as monotone as an out of work answering machine.

'Good morning. How can I help you, sir?'

I scanned his name badge. He didn't strike me as a Donald, but his hairstyle was pretty terrible.

'I want to pay my father's rent, please.'

Confusion spilt from his eyes. 'I'm sorry, sir; we no longer take rent payments at this building. Would you like me to give you a leaflet outlining our payment options?'

'When did you stop taking payments here?'

He handed me a leaflet without me asking for one.

'Six years ago.'

So where had the old man been paying his money? I grabbed the leaflet.

'If I give you his payment card, can you check how my father has been paying his rent?'

He appeared annoyed by the request, but the adage

about the customer always being right was stamped into his skull somewhere.

'Do you have his payment card?'

I handed it to him. He dragged it over a small terminal connected to his computer. It flashed a red light, and then he returned the card to me.

'Do you have the details?' I said.

'Can you confirm the name and address of the tenant?'

'Jack Walker, 49 Beach Road, Parish Hills. I'm his son, Frank.'

'Well, Mr Walker, your father has been paying his rent at the post office across from here. All the places he can pay are in the leaflet you have, including online and via the phone. He can also set up a direct debit.'

'Great.' He'd been paying at the post office all this time and forgotten to tell me. 'Thanks a lot, Donald.'

I went to leave, only to be stopped by someone calling my name.

'Mr Walker, can I have a word, please?'

I turned around to be greeted by a woman with a giant smile and the biggest glasses I'd seen outside of Elton John. She held her hand out to me. It was warm to the touch and I stared at her ID badge.

'What can I do for you, Carol Ann?'

She pointed at a door behind her. 'If you'll join me in here, I'll explain everything to you, Mr Walker.'

'Of course, but call me Frank. Mr Walker is my dad.'

She kept on smiling and I followed her into the room. It was as sterile as where I'd come from. There was a table and two chairs there. Carol Ann took one, and I sat in the other.

'Well, Frank, this is about your father.'

What had the old man done now? Or was he behind on his rent? Perhaps he'd forgotten to pay it.

'What's wrong, Carol Ann?'

'Oh, don't worry, Frank; he's done nothing wrong. I just wanted to remind him or get you to tell him he needs to come in and sign the paperwork if he intends to complete his option on our Right to Buy scheme.'

I nearly fell out of the chair when she said that. 'Right to Buy?'

'Yes. It allows most former council tenants to purchase their home at a discount.'

'I know what it is; what's that have to do with my father?'

'Well, since the property where he lives is now owned by Andreas Housing, and it was a council property when he first moved in, this is called Preserved Right to Buy. Your father spoke to me about it last month, wondering if he was eligible, and I wanted to tell him he is and he only needs to sign off on the scheme once we've talked about the discount he's entitled to and the method of payment.'

This couldn't be true. My mother had tried to convince him to buy the house for years, but he'd refused every time. And where would he get the money? As far as I was aware, he had limited savings.

'Can you tell me how much the discount is?'

Her teeth were as white as the walls. 'Even though you're his son, I can't talk about that without his written permission. What I will say is because your father has lived in the same house for over forty years, the discount he'd get would be substantial. He'd be able to buy the property for a fraction of its current market value.'

She seemed excited for him. I didn't know what to think.

I got out of the chair. 'Thank you for telling me, Carol Ann. I'll tell my father the good news as soon as possible.'

She thrust her hand out to me and I shook it again. Even though the room was as cold as a fridge, her skin was still warm. She escorted me out of the building. I let the wind brush my face and stared across the road, searching for the post office to pay this rent.

No matter how cheaply he could buy the house, why would he want to? If what she'd said was true, he'd started this process before I'd returned. He was intelligent enough to know he was close to the end of his life, and it was more than likely he'd have to live in a care home sooner rather than later.

So why would he want to buy the house he'd rented for over forty years?

I crossed the road, found the office, and paid the rent. Then I went to the supermarket and bought two bags worth of food.

The only thing occupying my mind, more so than a mysterious redheaded man out to get me, a missing neighbour, and a dead taxi driver, was why would my father want to buy that house?

15 SCHOOL DAYS

I dumped the shopping in the kitchen, leaving most of it on the side and placing the hot chicken and chips I'd bought on two plates. Then I took them into the living room.

We ate without speaking, everything still apart from the blare of the TV. The local news was full of George's murder and Dolores's disappearance. The national media hadn't caught on to it yet. As soon as they did, it wouldn't be long before the cameras and reporters would be outside the house. And if they found out I was living next door, was connected to these unfortunate neighbours, then it would burst into overdrive. I wasn't a celebrity, but someone would remember my name and connect all the dots sooner rather than later.

Perhaps I could move for a while.

I glanced over at the old man as he pulled chicken from his teeth. But where would I go? It wasn't as if I was burdened with cash for rented accommodation. That's why I'd come here in the first place, why I'd swallowed my pride, so I could save money before deciding what to do next. Some people, so-called friends and soon to be ex-colleagues, said I'd have no trouble finding a job in the private sector once I left the force, but all those promises had vanished in the wind once I'd quit. For some, police procedures meant more than catching a killer.

And what was this about the old man wanting to buy the house? He hadn't even asked me if I'd paid the rent when I got back, so I didn't broach the subject of him becoming a property owner. He finished his food and it was good to see him eating. I could only guess what he'd done for meals before I'd returned.

He smiled at me as I removed the plate – hunched over in his chair, leaning closer to the fake fire, edging his hands towards the lights coming from the bulbs behind the cover. I wondered if he knew it wasn't real. When I'd asked him why he had it switched on in the summer, he said it was because the replica flames made him feel as if he wasn't alone in this room, that he wasn't alone in this house.

Yet he had been since I'd left. I was the last to go. My mother had abandoned him when I turned sixteen, and my sisters had done the same when they reached that age. None of them had been in touch after that, as far as I knew.

Mary, at sixty-six, was the oldest, while my other sister, Colleen, was a year younger. Because of the age difference and their desperation to get away, I'd never met either of them. I'd read the letters they'd sent my mother, overheard them on phone calls, but that was it. Growing up, I thought that's how all families were, that it was normal to be like that, especially with the gap in years between us, and it was a test of strength, a test of character.

My brother and I had had a frosty relationship. I was

twelve when he joined the army, not fully understanding what was happening and that he wouldn't be back. I gained my taste in music and love of reading from the records and books he left behind.

But that was as close as we got; we had no deep and meaningful conversations, no talks about our unemotional parents. I suppose those things would have been impossible for a twelve-year-old and a young man not much more than a kid himself. It seems a terrible thing to say, but Tommy wasn't the brightest. I might have skipped most of my last two years at school, but it wasn't because I lacked intelligence and had more to do with boredom. The bright lights in other parts of the country were more educational than dusty textbooks and teachers who wanted to be somewhere else.

Tommy was different to me in that respect; he was slower to pick things up and found it difficult to hold conversations. Unlike me, he didn't have many friends, and I never saw him with a girlfriend. Even at twelve, with my height and physique, I had no problems on that score.

The military appealed to my brother, even if our father had tried to dissuade him from joining. But Tommy didn't listen. The last I'd heard, he'd left the army and disappeared into the throng of the British population.

These types of memories, of a family in name only, were fleeting thoughts in the time I'd lived in London, but now they were returning to me in a rush and at the most inappropriate times. Being back in this house, close to him, must have been what was doing it. So again, I asked myself if I should move out to find another job, any job.

I peered at my father, who was transfixed by the doppelgänger of nature warming the room. The light from the flames illuminated his tired, worn face, wrinkles boring into his skin. His expression was of weariness and defeat.

He turned those exhausted eyes to mine. 'What will you do about Thompson?'

I didn't know whether to laugh or cry. I'd forgotten all about my old friend, the Toenail. No doubt he or his cronies would visit me at some point, but I figured he wouldn't do anything rash just yet, not with the added police interest in me and what had happened to my neighbours. Tony was never the brightest, but I wouldn't put it past him to be busy plotting how to make my life the most miserable it could be.

Did I make his life, and others, a misery – as bad as he'd claimed? I'd forgotten about the Frank the Butcher nickname the kids had given me, but I was sure, even with a hazy memory, he must have been exaggerating. And he'd always been a compulsive liar.

'He won't trouble us, Dad.' That word didn't sound any easier on my tongue. 'Not with the police snooping around the estate. And I've got more important things to do.'

I removed the paper from my pocket, the one with Grace's address on it. It was light outside, but I'd changed my plan to wait until after dark to visit her. My curiosity was burning through me and I couldn't wait any longer. After my trip to the housing office and the shops had gone without incident, I assumed none of the locals would bother me.

'You're going to see Grace about him, this Harpo bloke?'

The sofa creaked under my legs as I stood.

'I might as well do it now.' I handed him the remote for the TV. 'You stay here and don't let anyone in unless it's the police. There's more food in the kitchen if you get hungry and a few cans of cider in the fridge if you fancy a drink.'

His wrinkled face crumpled as he rubbed at it, his

spotted fingers flickering in the artificial light like domino dots, desperate to find the perfect match. As I got to the door, his voice was croaky as he spoke.

'Be careful, son.'

I would have sworn there was a single tear in his eye as I left. I had to ask him about this house buying business when I returned. He wouldn't be purchasing it for himself; it made little sense. Was it possible, just maybe, that one or more of my wayward siblings had been in touch with him? Four weeks ago, I'd have said that was impossible, but four weeks ago, I would have said there was more chance of me winning the lottery than being in my current situation.

The air was warm as I stepped out of the house. It didn't matter what had happened with Thompson, the police, and the Cooks; I finally had something to go on with Grace's note and invitation. Of course, Dolores's disappearance concerned me, but this was the best way of finding her.

I strode past the pub, peering through the window to see someone else working behind the bar, before turning the corner to the street where the primary school was. There were already several adults milling around, waiting for the kids to finish their educational day.

They were mainly women, probably only half a dozen men amongst the sixty or so who strode through the gates into the playground. I followed them and waited for my memories of the building to return. I'd disliked secondary school because of the tedium, but I'd always thought kindly of this place.

Apart from one particular person: the Cow of Parish Primary, the kids had called her. This was the Head Teacher, Mrs Bullock. She was stern and horrible and as unforgiven as anyone I'd ever met, including murderers and

serial killers. She'd believed education could only be prac-
tised by physically and emotionally hurting the children.

Unfortunately for many, England didn't ban corporal
punishment in state schools until 1986, and by then, I was
well out of Mrs Bullock's reach. But she left one lasting
memory with me: when I was nine or ten, I sprinted from
the house – I can never remember why – and ran across a
busy road. A double-decker bus missed hitting me by a fraction, while a car coming the other way had to swerve up
onto the pavement to avoid me. I didn't wait around to see
the results, my trembling legs taking me off the estate and
down towards the beck and the railway lines.

It was the following morning when I discovered the
consequences of my actions. It had been Bullock driving the
car that had just missed me, and she ensured the whole
school knew how stupid and irresponsible I'd been. She got
me in front of everyone at assembly, recounted what had
happened, and then instructed me to tell the whole school
what a terrible child I was. Only I refused to do that, staying
silent no matter how many times she threatened to punish
me with the cane.

Instead, she made me stand in the corner, face to the
wall, for the rest of the morning. Three hours I stood there,
only released when I could go for my dinner – people call it
lunch now, but it was always dinner to us. Then she
returned me to the same spot until school finished for the
day. She sent a letter home to my parents about my
behaviour, but they didn't speak about it.

But they never talked about anything: there was no
response from them when the police grabbed me and a
bunch of other kids for throwing stones at passing trains; no
response when I was caught shoplifting; no reaction when a

neighbour's son said I stole his pocket money; no response when kids called me a bully.

I paused inside the school gates, trying to put all those returning memories into the right place. I wasn't a bully – I only stood up for myself against the older kids, and the stolen pocket money was me fighting for what they'd taken from me.

I moved past the school and towards the field at the rear. It wasn't only to avoid the other adults, but also to drown out the memory of Bullock and that day I nearly caused her to crash. The front of the building had a fancy new façade, but the classrooms appeared to be the same as when I was there in the dark ages. I didn't hang around. A fence separated the field and the houses on the other side as I strode across the grass towards Grace's house.

It was only as I reached the fence that I remembered houses rarely have numbers at the back, so I wouldn't be able to work out which was 49.

My hand slammed against the wood, sending splinters into my palm. I ignored the pain and chastised myself for my stupidity. That's when I saw each yard had the blue and green council bins ready to collect the right rubbish on the right day; bins with numbers on them, and the one I was looking at was 37.

I moved alongside the fence, counting inside my head in case I didn't see the bins for her house, but I needn't have worried: two white 49s painted on blue and green flashed across my retinas. I clambered over the fence and into the yard. It was a smaller place than where my father lived, with overgrowing weeds, pots of dead flowers, and the stink of unwashed dogs.

The back door was straight ahead. I moved towards it without thinking how I'd get inside. The curtains were closed. My hand was on the door when it creaked open. There was broken glass on the floor and the smell of coffee drifting over me.

After what had happened at the Cooks' house, with Dolores's semi-invite and an open door waiting for me, did I want to do this again?

What choice did I have?

16 ART ATTACK

I shut the door when I got inside. The noisy hum of a refrigerator welcomed me into the house, last year's calendar askew on a nail, with a wobbly three-legged table sitting in the middle of a grease-splattered floor. It smelt of fried eggs as I avoided the mess. Someone had broken a glass as dark liquid slithered over the floor, so I stepped over it towards the gap leading into the corridor.

Before I headed into the living room, a loud noise exploded from upstairs. This was *déjà vu*. Common sense told me to get out, but I'd never been known for following that instinct. As I put my hand on the bannister, a large book bounced downstairs to land at my feet.

I stepped over the cover, Enid Blyton's *Famous Five* gazing up at me as I took the stairs two at a time. Should I call out to Grace to see if she was okay? If I was still a copper, I would have; but I wasn't, and my intuition told me I was walking into a trap.

Yet I continued, reaching the top with no other noises or flying novels. The bathroom was ahead of me, the door open to show it was empty. There were rooms on either side.

I went into the first one, scanning every inch of the place. There was an unmade bed with discarded clothes strewn across the floor. A dark jacket similar to the one Grace had worn in the pub was hanging on the back of a chair, next to a small table covered in glossy magazines featuring the latest celebrity gossip. Light streamed through the curtains, and the place smelt of hairspray and deodorant. Art deco prints were on the walls, images of glamorous people enjoying stylish destinations.

I strode past a wardrobe and into the corridor. There was one room left and the door was closed. I tested the bottom with my foot, inching it forward to see inside. It was like the other bedroom, slightly larger, with the same type of furniture and a mirror on the back wall. The big difference was the body on the bed.

The floorboards creaked as I approached Grace, hoping she was only asleep. I tried to be quiet so as not to wake her, then realised how stupid that was since I was there to speak to her. As I got closer, I noticed the marks on her neck, horrible purple welts that were the unmistakable indents of human fingers.

A footstep behind me forced my gaze up from the dreadful sight to a shock of curly red hair caught in the bedroom mirror hanging over Grace's unmoving frame. Then, before I could turn, something battered into the back of my skull. I stumbled forward, knees hitting the edge of the bed, my hand on the sheets as my legs gave way.

I tried to push up, but was hit again, losing sight of my attacker to focus on the bronze statue of a woman draped in a cape with her arms outstretched. One of her stiff fingers cut across my face, the blood dripping over the carpet as I thudded to the floor. I twisted my head, my blurred vision burning my eyes as that red hair shone above me.

That was all I could see, unable to focus or hear anything but the thumping inside my skull. That ruby mane hung closer to me, his breath heavy and wheezy.

Was it a man? I couldn't tell in my current state.

It might have been a large woman.

My attacker lifted the weapon, looking ready to place it one last time in the middle of my face. I waited for it to land as all the strength vanished from me. Then the room went black as the bronze woman readied to throw herself into my skull.

———

THE SMELL of ammonia hit me when I woke. My eyes continued to sting, but at least I could see correctly. I sat up in the bed, staring around the hospital room, and noticed my father snoozing in the corner. Next to him were a uniformed police officer and DS Smith.

Her voice made my head hurt again.

'He's awake, DI Rose. Shall I cuff him now?'

Sara Rose marched into the room. 'There's no need for that, Deb. Mr Walker is an innocent for once.'

She grabbed a chair and sat opposite me.

'How is Grace?' My throat croaked and burnt at the same time.

'Unfortunately, she drifted into a coma not long after she got to the hospital. The doctors say it will be touch and go if she ever recovers, and even if she does, there's a chance she'll have a brain injury.'

I wiped the sweat from my forehead using trembling hands. My father was awake and staring at me, but I couldn't face him, turning to Rose instead.

'Did she mention who attacked her?'

Rose shook her head, the curls of her dark hair falling to her shoulders.

'She didn't say much on the way to the hospital, but she told the paramedics you saved her life. That and those nasty bruises to the back of your head and your face convinced me of your innocence in this attack.'

'But not the others?'

I had a sudden urge to go to the toilet, but I held it in. I wouldn't show these people my trembling body in a hospital gown that was far too small for me.

'We're still investigating the murder of George Cross and the disappearance of his wife.'

'You haven't found Dolores?'

The longer she was missing, the worse it was likely to be.

'Not for want of trying. But now we can tie George's death to the attack on Grace Marsh.'

'You've got evidence the same person strangled them?'

'It's looking that way.'

'So, I'm off the hook then?'

It was some good news. Rose didn't take long to dash that thought.

'Well, I still think you're involved and are keeping things from us, keeping information from me.'

Her knees touched the side of the bed and I got a whiff of her perfume. Perhaps I was still dizzy from the bangs on the head, but my mind drifted into places it shouldn't regarding Detective Inspector Sara Rose.

I gave her my best smile. 'You've got me all wrong, Inspector.'

'So why were you at Grace's house? Was this another case of you playing white night to a damsel in distress?'

'I sent him there.'

My father's voice sounded how I felt – broken and discouraged.

Rose turned to him. 'You'll need to explain that to me in more detail, Mr Walker.'

He grinned at her. 'You can call me Jack, love. Frank went to Grace's house because she told me to send him there.'

'Why did you do that, Jack?'

'Because she gave me the name of the redheaded man who's trying to frame him.'

He was tired, but there was clarity to his words I hadn't recognised since my return.

'When did she tell you this?'

I could only see the back of her head, but I imagined how mesmerising her eyes would be to him. Hell, I was smitten by the sound of her voice, and I couldn't even see her face.

'Last night after she took me home from the pub, before you and your gang arrived to annoy Thompson. Grace told me she'd seen this man before, though not with the Cooks. She'd spoken to him in the bar a few weeks before and his name was Harpo.'

'Just like the silent Marx Brother,' DI Rose said.

I flipped my legs over the side of the bed, not caring if she saw me like that. She gazed into my eyes.

'I didn't realise you were a connoisseur of classic Hollywood movies, Inspector Rose.'

'My grandfather loved the Marx Brothers, Chaplin, and Laurel and Hardy. We used to watch those together when he was in the hospice.'

Sadness possessed her eyes, and I didn't know what to say. Finally, it was my father who ended the awkward silence.

'So what happens now, Inspector?'

As she stood, her hand glanced against my side, and even through the hospital gown, I felt the touch of her skin. My head was fuzzy and I lay on the bed, my legs naked from the knees down, my heart beating as if a heavy metal drummer was using it to make terrible music.

'Officers will be stationed outside Ms Marsh's room and here.'

She peered at me and I'd never felt so weak in my life. It was a struggle to get the words out.

'There's no need for that. I'll be leaving here soon.'

I lifted my body, shoulders shaking, my breath coming in painful bursts. She placed her hand on my arm.

'That's not a good idea, Frank. The doctors said you need at least another twenty-four hours here to make sure you don't have a concussion.' Her smile warmed every inch of me. 'You'd be no good to anybody wandering around outside in this state.'

She was right, and I'd be a sitting duck for another attack, and not just from Harpo. But I couldn't abandon my father. He was more vulnerable than me to those who wanted to harm me.

'I can't leave my dad on his own, Rose.'

I placed my hand on hers, not to remove it, but to steady myself and prove how determined I was. That smile just kept on coming, her energy making me feel a lot better.

'I figured you'd say that, Frank. So I arranged for your father to have a room next to you for this night, at least. I'll be back tomorrow to reassess the situation.'

The gratitude and sense of relief nearly overwhelmed me. I took her fingers and squeezed them.

'Thank you, Inspector.'

She leant into my face and that perfume was like laudanum swimming inside my skull.

'It's my pleasure, Frank, and you can call me Sara when the grunts aren't around. Speaking of which,' she let go of me and turned to her colleagues, 'DS Smith will get your dad settled, and I'll sort out the uniformed protection for you and Grace. I'll return to see you both tomorrow.'

With that, she was out of the room, taking my heart with her. DS Smith guided the old man out, and I slid my weary legs under the sheets. I attributed this sudden attraction to Rose to my ordeal and whatever drugs the doctors had pumped into me.

I lay my head on the pillow. I was sad for what had happened to Grace, but at least DI Rose now knew I was innocent and that Harpo was real; the police could concentrate on finding him while I rested up. And maybe, with my father in the room next door, there might be a chance to see a specialist here who could give me some advice on the state of the old man's mental facilities.

The pillow was comfier than I'd expected, its soft exterior sucking out the swamp in my brain. Then someone slapped me across my face. My eyes flicked open in shock, seeing DS Smith standing over me.

'Don't get too comfortable, Walker. You might have dodged one problem, but you've got a bigger one to deal with.'

'What are you talking about?'

She placed a card on the bedside table. 'You need to go to that address at ten o'clock tomorrow night.'

'Why would I do that?'

'Mr Thompson wants to have an urgent conversation with you.'

If I'd had the strength, I'd have laughed at her.

'Tony the Toenail? What makes you think I'd go anywhere to see that ratbag?'

She made her way to the door, turning to me.

'Because if you don't, then how else will your old man be able to pay the twenty grand in gambling debts he owes Mr Thompson?'

As she left, I wondered if I was still in Grace's bedroom, being beaten over the head by a curly redheaded lunatic wielding an art deco statue.

17 SISTER MORPHINE

Fizzy pop sparkled through a paper straw as I drank from a plastic cup. It bubbled inside my stomach, bouncing around like drunken ants at an insect disco. I'd finished my hospital meal, which I was reluctant to describe as food considering how poor it was: eggs so watery they could have supported the Ark and ham paler and tougher than an albino rhinoceros. At least the sugar from the drink drowned out the taste of the food.

I got out of bed and shuffled from the room, still uncomfortable in the hospital gown designed for someone half my size. My police protection – not Tony Thompson's uniformed nark – eyed me as I reached the corridor. I pointed to the room next to mine.

'I'm just popping in to see my father.'

The copper nodded and watched me doing my best impersonation of a man twice my age. I lifted my fingers to the back of my neck, unsurprised at how quickly the bruises had erupted into small mountains on my flesh. I assumed they were a vibrant colour of blue and purple.

The air had an unpolluted fragrance, not sterile, just

clean, with the corridor leading off to the wards, where about a dozen patients were in individual beds. This wasn't the hospital I had been born in, but the one where I'd had my appendix removed before it threatened to burst. It was the place where doctors had stuck a needle into the back of my throat in an emergency procedure to remove my toxic tonsils before they exploded inside my mouth.

I pushed the door open and found my father, fully dressed in that suit, in a chair with a battered copy of a Len Deighton book on his lap. There was a photo of the Brandenburg Gate in Berlin on the cover, all lit up at night and glistening in gold.

The old man's eyes were also sparkling. I wondered if he read books like that to remind him of his travels abroad before his marriage. My father had never mentioned the part he played in the war or the terrible things he must have witnessed, endured, and possibly participated in. The snippets I knew about had always come from my mother. I think it was her way of excusing or rationalising his behaviour.

'He was never like this before he went to war,' was her mantra when he fell into the trap of his worst vice: a vice I thought he'd escaped from. But, if DS Smith wasn't lying to wind me up, it would seem he'd sunk further into that vice than ever before.

I didn't move from the doorway. 'Do you owe Tony Thompson money?'

His fingers were like crooked branches as they clutched at the book.

'It's none of your business.'

'It is when I'm getting dodgy coppers telling me I have to meet Thompson about your debts.'

My voice was harsher than I intended it to sound, but there was no choice – his gambling and what it did to us had always disgusted me. Perhaps this was the last straw, and I'd move out of his house for the second and final time.

The wrinkles covering his face vibrated as he glared at me.

'All coppers are dodgy.'

I didn't know if that was a dig at my previous life or about the police here, or perhaps a bit of both.

'Has this got something to do with you buying the house?'

His lips trembled as he gazed at me, grim blueish lines amid his stubble. He dropped the book to the floor, his anguished eyes cutting into mine. His voice was a slow whisper.

'Who told you that?'

'A woman at Andreas Housing mentioned it when I went to pay your rent. She said you're eligible under their scheme and would get a considerable discount because you've lived in the house for so long. The papers are there waiting for you; they only need your signature.'

He appeared to be at a loss for words, the flesh of his face rippling as if he was underwater. He gazed at me, then found what he wanted to say.

'Thompson said he'd write off my debts if I did it. So I could still live there, but I'd have to sign the house over to one of his companies.'

My head spun as if it was inside a washing machine.

'Why does Thompson want your house?'

'I don't know, Frank, but I wouldn't do it, anyway. He can take a flying flip for his money. What's the worst he can do to me?'

'He'll stop you from gambling, and because I'm assuming you're not visiting legal betting shops, you'll keep going back to him to get what you need.' He couldn't help himself. I don't know why I'd forgotten that. I guess old age doesn't necessarily always bring wisdom with it.

He was hunched over in the chair, his eyes seeping into the book at his feet. Was this what his life had come to, after surviving the D-Day landings, fighting across Europe, and witnessing the horrors of the Holocaust? To return a broken man unable to connect with anyone, especially his wife and children, and end up at the mercy of his addictions and some low-life wannabe gang-lord?

As a kid, I'd never perceived my father as an addict, neither for his everyday drinking nor for the gambling. However, once I moved to London, joined the force and encountered addicts and their dealers, not to mention numerous social workers and psychologists, I thought differently about his behaviour.

It wasn't a regular thing for me to dwell on his habits that negatively affected the family. Still, the memories would occasionally reappear when I worked on cases involving drugs or alcohol addiction. For example, one psychologist who worked with the police had an interesting theory about addiction based on contemporary studies. She told me that if we gave a bunch of people heroin for twenty days straight, we'd all expect to know the outcome. We'd think because there are chemical hooks in heroin, the body would become dependent on those hooks, would need them physically, and at the end of those twenty days, every one of those people would be addicts.

Then she told me many people are given hard drugs in hospitals, including heroin substitutes, but they don't come out as addicts. You don't see grannies with new hips pretending they're extras from *Trainspotting* and searching for drug dealers once they've been discharged from the hospital, do you?

Those people are exposed to all those chemical hooks in hospitals, so they should become addicts, but they don't. So why don't they? Well, she claimed that addiction is a reaction to your environment, and there have been legitimate academic studies on this. They don't even label it an addiction; they call it bonding. It's a connection.

And humans have a natural desire to bond. That's when we're happy and healthy. We'll bond and connect, but if we can't do that because we're distressed or isolated or frazzled, we'll bond with something else to ease the pressure on us. Now, that might be alcohol or drugs, pornography, or collecting model trains; it could be a sports team or the works of Lee Child or Katy Perry, but we'll bond and connect with something because it's in our nature. That's what we want as human beings.

I listened to her, taking some of it in but dismissing most as just another excuse for dreadful people doing horrible things out of greed or hate. But now, as I watched my father's eyes fill with water, it made perfect sense to me. Here was a man raised in terrible poverty and social deprivation, shunted off into a global conflict while still a teenager, who witnessed the worst of human behaviour; who came back and tried to be a regular husband and father while unable to speak to anyone about what he'd experienced.

They called it shellshock after World War I. Now we know it as Post Traumatic Stress Disorder, and I realised my father was still living through his shock and disorder. I didn't understand why he couldn't get the connection he needed with his wife and children, why he couldn't find any relationship with me or his other children, but perhaps his addictions all came from that; and if that was the case, how could I leave him to fend for himself now?

Tears filled his face. I remembered my humanity, not as a son, but as a person, and went to him. His fingers were cold in mine, and I thought the light behind his eyes might flicker out and die.

'What shall I do, Frank?'

He wasn't asking me for advice; he was looking for salvation and a way out of this mess. I let go of one of his hands and removed the card with Thompson's address on it. I showed it to my old man.

'Do you know where this is?'

He wiped his face. 'It's hard to see without my magnifying glass.'

I read it to him. '166 Stone Road, Bridge End. Is this where Thompson lives?'

He thought for a second, and then the sparkle returned to his eyes.

'It's what used to be that pub, The Golden Lion.'

The memories came back to me in a flash. It was on a neighbouring estate, but some of us would drink there when we were fifteen and sixteen. It was a proper dive and an easy place to get served when you shouldn't have been there legally. And, if I remembered correctly, they'd had the nicest looking barmaids. I'm sure one of my earliest sexual experiences was in the backroom of that pub.

'Is it closed down now?'

The old pub was set away from the main road, leading into the grass and the beck close to it; on the other side was the train line.

'It has been for years, but Thompson runs some of his operations from there.' The old man appeared guilty as he spoke. 'I've never been there. I only used the gambling booths he set up in the Slaughtered Lamb after the pub was shut.'

'What type of betting were you involved in, Dad?'

I tried to sound as sympathetic as possible.

'Mainly cards; sometimes they'd put live dog racing on the TV from China or the Philippines.'

I looked at him, needing to know how he'd accumulated twenty grand's worth of debts to a scumbag like Thompson. But I didn't ask, helping him get undressed and into bed. Then I said goodnight and went to my room.

I gazed at the card with the address on it. I'd known there'd be another meeting with Thompson at some point, but I thought I'd be able to put it off until I found this Harpo guy who had it in for me. Yet Thompson had made it clear he had it in for me as well, and what was the likelihood two different people would do that when I returned to the family home after twenty-five years away?

I switched off the light and touched the bruises on the back of my head again. Thompson had exploited my old man, and some other nut job had killed others to get to me. I didn't know how or when it would happen, but I knew that both of them were going to pay for it.

18 I FOUGHT THE LAW

I was up early and dressed when DI Rose knocked on my door. I offered her some coffee the nurse had brought me earlier, and it was good to see her grin.

'No thanks, Frank. I've had hospital coffee before, and it's about as tasteful as drinking mucus.'

'You've got some experience of drinking mucus?'

'No, but I have a vivid imagination. So how was your night in the luxury of the NHS?'

I finished the coffee with a grimace; she wasn't far wrong about the taste.

'Everyone working here doesn't get paid enough. Is this a social visit?'

Rose scrunched her eyes and laughed. 'You're not my type, Frank, so don't be getting any ideas on that front.' My early morning bonhomie vanished in an instant. 'I've brought you news about the Midnight Strangler.'

'Is that what you're calling Harpo?'

She shook her head. 'It's not my idea. I'm sure you know how coppers hate giving criminals fancy names; this one is straight from the media.'

'And it's inaccurate since neither of the attacks happened at midnight.'

'I've found it best never to imagine the media as possessing anything more than limited intellects.' She grabbed a chair and sat down. 'I need a rest. It's only nine o'clock, and already my feet ache.' She was wearing sensible shoes, but had my sympathy. 'How are the bumps on your head?'

I lifted my fingers to them, feeling a pinch as I pressed.

'Still there and still hurting. As long as I don't enjoy myself, I should be okay.'

Her eyebrows flickered as if they were butterflies trying to get away from her face.

'Do you want to hear my opinion of you, Frank, as one detective to a former detective?'

I slumped onto the bed as the memory of the coffee made me shiver.

'I'm one ginormous ear waiting for you.'

She removed a phone from her pocket and placed it on the bedside table where I'd left the card with Thompson's address on it. I glanced at her, then the card, then back to her.

'I've spoken to a few more of your ex-colleagues since our strangler attacked you, and they told me quite a few interesting things.'

I bet they did. 'Do I want to know what they think of me? Too many people worry about what others think about them when they should focus on believing in themselves.'

Rose clapped her hands together. 'That's what most of them said about you: that you were a great copper, one of the best they'd ever seen. You're intelligent, but it's your self-confidence, some would say arrogance, which pushed you into solving crimes many others couldn't. You never give up, and you never back down, and you one hundred per cent hate it when the guilty get away.'

'You're not telling me anything new here, Rose.'

Could I grab the card without her noticing? Maybe if I kept her talking. She appeared to like the sound of her own voice. I was hoping she talked too much when she was attracted to someone.

'The first time I saw you, you'd just been accused of beating up your neighbours. The second time was in the pub with a gangster who hates you. When we took you away, I told you about the murder and the disappearance of those same neighbours. Then we find you on the floor of a woman who'd been strangled, and you'd been attacked.'

Her hand was on the table, her fingers close to the card.

'Is this your version of "Previously on the Frank Walker show"?'

'Despite all this going on with you, and what I heard from your former colleagues, you come across as the calmest of seas, but there's always motion under the water, always something going on we can't see; and I'm wondering what your motion is and when it'll show itself.'

I dragged my gaze from the table.

'That's fascinating, Rose, but I don't believe you came all the way here just to tell me that.'

She grabbed her phone, knocking the card to the floor near her feet.

'No wonder you were such a good detective, Frank.' She flicked her fingers across the screen. 'Forensics came up with some interesting observations overnight; would you like to hear what they are?'

She lurched forward a little, her left foot inching over the card.

'Sure; what else have I got to do?'

The card was under her shoe.

'Our unknown assailant was sitting behind George in the taxi and grabbed him by the throat. Cross died of compression of the neck.'

'Strangulation.'

'Yes; it appears as if our killer wore leather gloves as fibres were found in George's skin and under his fingers.'

'He tried to pull his attacker off him.'

'The pressure must have been too much for George to do anything.' She showed me the image on her phone of the marks on George's throat. Then she took it away and changed it to another photo. 'This happened to Grace.' The wounds were the same. 'It looks as if she was sleeping when our attacker snuck into the bedroom. Then he got on the bed and knelt over her. She'd have died if you hadn't entered the house and distracted the perp.'

That didn't make me feel any better. 'This is all standard stuff, no?'

'Well, that's what I thought until forensics pointed out what I'd missed the first time I examined the images.'

She reduced the size and put them side by side on the screen to show me.

'They're too small for me to see anything significant.'

Rose shook her head and changed the screen again.

'Here, I increased the size on Cook's photo. What do you notice?'

I took the phone from her, got up, and moved to the other side of the room. Perhaps I could get her away from the card and retrieve it without her seeing it.

'The indentations from the fingers are unusual on the right of his neck, lighter than the other side.' I pulled the screen closer to my face. 'It's as if all the pressure came from the left hand.' I turned to her. 'Our killer must be left-handed?'

'It looks that way. Can I have my phone back?'

I held it in both of my hands. Then I threw it onto the bed using my right hand.

'Was this a test to see if I'm left-handed?'

She smiled at me, but didn't move.

'Don't be silly, Frank.' She narrowed her eyes. 'Is this paranoia the motion under your calm exterior?'

I stepped towards the door. 'I'm going to collect my father.'

She got up and reached for her phone. My knees creaked as I snatched the card from the floor, holding it between my fingers as she turned to me.

'Do you want me to leave a police car outside your house?'

'Now who's being silly? The locals would set it alight before the day was out, and you don't have the people to spare.' I slipped the card into my back pocket. 'I can look after myself, but thanks for being so concerned.'

'So, what's next for you?'

I wouldn't lie to her. 'I'll take the old man home and wait for the police to catch a killer.'

'We still haven't found Dolores.'

That was a knife in my heart. I recognised she'd played me and set me up, but was it my fault she was missing? The longer it took to locate her, the worse it was likely to be. But perhaps I could do something about it; maybe I could find her. If anyone knew what happened on the estate, then surely it was its so-called protector, Tony Thompson?

Now I had two reasons to see him.

I placed my hand on Rose's arm, happy she didn't flinch or grimace.

'You'll find her and the killer, Sara.'

I left her and went into my father's room. He was already dressed and waiting for me, sitting in that same chair, reading his book. His walking stick was next to him.

'How are we getting home, Frank?'

I dug into my pockets to retrieve the last of my cash. How much remained in my bank account? There couldn't be a lot.

'We'll get a taxi, Dad.'

As we departed the hospital, I thanked all the staff who'd helped us. Rose wandered into the room where Grace Marsh was sleeping. I took out my phone and rang for the taxi. The old man was quiet as we waited, both of us watching people going in and out of the building. I wondered if he thought about how long he had left. And whether he considered his past much. How much of his past could he even remember?

'Can we have a curry when we get back?'

He was hungry, so that was a good sign. But, unfortunately, my lack of cash wasn't.

'Of course; we'll have curry, chips and rice once the takeaway opens.' That would be in another three hours. So there was plenty of time for me to develop a plan for walking into Tony Thompson's lion's den.

'What are you going to do about Thompson?'

There was concern in his eyes, but I wasn't sure if it was for me or his predicament. I removed the card from my pocket and stared at the address. There was dirt on it from Rose's foot. I didn't wipe it off.

'I'll go there tonight and speak to him. Don't worry about it, Dad.'

'Should I sign the house over to him?'

He'd forgotten about his outburst from yesterday,

promising not to give Toenail anything. I gazed at him as if he was the child and I was his father.

'These gambling sessions of his you went to, were they illegal?'

He nodded as his lips trembled. 'Most of them were, yes.'

I'd seen this sort of fix in London. 'Did you win the first few times you played?'

The memory of it made him smile. 'I won big, two or three thousand at least.'

'He suckered you in and knew you'd come back for more. Then, once you started losing and continued to lose, he lent you the money and allowed you to play with markers, didn't he?'

His eyes flared red. 'I was stupid.'

I put my hand on his shoulder as the taxi pulled up.

'No, Dad, you weren't. People like Thompson prey on the communities they infest. You're old and not in the best of health, and he took advantage of you.'

'So what will you say to him?'

I rubbed the bruises on the back of my head.

'I'll tell him to stick his threats up his arse, and he can whistle for his money. He broke the law, not you.'

His hand was on the top of the car, one trembling leg in the vehicle.

'Won't he set his thugs on you?'

I helped him inside. 'I'm sure he'll try, but even though he has the muscle, I have something he and people like him don't have.'

'What's that?'

'Brains,' I said as I shut the door and got into the passenger seat.

All I had to do now was use those brains to work out

how to get Thompson to help me find Dolores and Harpo while convincing him to write off the old man's debts and not beat me into a bloody pulp.

No problem.

19 FOOD FOR THOUGHT

I arranged for the same taxi driver to return to the house and pick me up at nine-fifty. He had me outside the former Golden Lion pub just before ten o'clock. I'd gone to the cash machine in the afternoon and removed the last of my savings. I would need to ask him for a loan soon, my ninety-three-year-old father, who was in debt to the man I'd come to see for twenty grand. Wasn't it strange how life could change in such a short space of time? It wasn't so long ago I was wining and dining in some of London's finest joints, and now here I was on my uppers on my way to some shit-hole in the north with no idea of what I was getting into.

A rickety metal fence surrounded the pub apart from a narrow gap around the back, but I couldn't get through that. I put my hand on it and a section fell away, tumbling to the ground with a clang and awaking a horde of dogs somewhere in the shadows. They howled as if it was the end of the world. If I'd planned to get in quietly and discreetly, it was already up shit creek.

I ignored the racket and strode to the back door, stepping over broken glass, disused needles and empty kebab boxes. The place stank like a rubbish tip. I approached a wall covered in obscene graffiti and got an intense blast of sweat as I banged on the entrance. After that, I didn't see any point in trying to be subtle anymore.

Nothing happened for a good three minutes apart from the dogs squawking even louder. Then, somewhere to my right, came the noise of the wind rippling through the beck. I hammered on the wood again, wondering if they had set me up and some of Thompson's goons would run around the corner with baseball bats in their hands.

I was about to give up and go when the door swung open and a teenage girl dressed like one of the Adams Family peered at me. Had I stumbled into an underage Goth party by mistake?

'Are you Walker?'

Her voice sounded as if it had been filtered through a thousand cigarettes. The pure whiteness of her teeth was in stark contrast to the black consuming the rest of her appearance.

'Is Thompson here?'

'He's waiting for you.'

She turned from me and went inside, so I followed her. I hadn't come just to give up at the last minute. It was dark inside, but there was enough moonlight shining through the broken roof for me to get a good sight of it, seeing it was nothing like the place I'd drunk and snogged in such a long time ago.

The building seemed to shudder as the wind battered the outsides. Beams stretched high overhead, and dust dripped down through cracks in the roof. We walked through what had been the back bar of the pub, with decrepit pool tables lining the far side of the wall.

The girl came to a door and pushed it open. Light blared through the gap and dazzled my eyes. I stepped behind her into a different world: where the last room was dark and dead, this was alive and buzzing. There was a gang of blokes in the corner, some of whom were Thompson's goons from the other night; it wasn't them that interested me, but what was to my left.

There was a large standing sign with Community Food Bank stamped on it. All around it were boxes of provisions people must have donated. I was confused as to why they were there. Was Thompson that low he'd stolen things provided for the needy?

'The look on your face is precious.'

I turned to see him, a man with the forlorn insincerity of a Shopping Channel presenter, grinning at me as if he was Father Christmas come early.

'Is this another one of your scams, Tony?'

He placed a hand on his heart in mock tragedy.

'You wound me, Frank; you do. Are there no pure thoughts in that twisted head of yours?'

'I know you've likely built a career out of being wrong about almost everything, so I'm not sure what it is you're doing here, but I'd guess the only person it benefits is you.'

'You didn't listen to me the other day in the pub, did you?' He removed his expensive jacket and hung it on the back of a shabby chair. Then he held his hand out to me. 'I need to apologise to you about the Slaughtered Lamb. I was upset with what happened between you and Phil, and I let my parental love get the better of me. I'm sorry, Frank.'

My mouth must have opened wide enough to catch a swarm of locusts, so they flew in to buzz inside my confused brain. He pushed his hand closer to me and, without realising it, I took it. His grip was rugged, and he shook vigorously before letting go. This wasn't what I'd expected at all. He grinned at my confusion.

I pointed to the sign. 'Why are these boxes of food and drinks in here?'

The grin disappeared from his face. 'Did you know that last year, one in fifty households used a food bank, and ninety-four per cent of people using them were destitute? They couldn't afford to eat, be clothed, or get clean. And that almost three-quarters of people who use food banks live in households struggling with ill health or disability, and one in ten has a learning disability?'

I'd seen what years of government austerity had done to the most vulnerable in the country, but wasn't aware of the figures. They were shocking, but I was just as dazed that Thompson told me this with such sorrow in his voice.

'You're involved with distributing this to those who need it most?'

'If people like me don't, who will? Not the government, that's for sure.' The look on his face had transformed from sadness to anger. 'The thing about the normalisation of hardship is it's only a matter of time before something which once horrified the country is allowed to get worse.' He walked to one box and picked out a tin of beans. 'Communities like ours have to look after ourselves, and people in those communities, ones with connections and the right worldview, will deliver what is needed. This is what I was trying to tell you the other night.'

He dropped the tin back into the box.

'I think the threat of violence may have confused the issue, Tony.'

Since we were friends again, I thought it prudent to be back on first-name terms. At least until I found out how this scam of his worked.

'Once more, Frank, I apologise for that.'

He didn't hold out his hand. Whatever game he was playing, it was time to dispense with it and get down to why I was there.

'Does my father owe you twenty thousand pounds?'

He put his hands together and summoned up his best politician's expression, the one where the eyes and the mouth move, but you know whatever is inside his head is going in the opposite direction.

'Ah, yes. I'm afraid that's true.'

'If you're such a man of the people, Tone, why would you let an old man get into such debt?'

'It was an error for it to increase so much, Frank. I'll admit that. But, if we believe in free will, shouldn't we allow others to make mistakes?'

I puffed out my chest and resisted the urge to punch his lights out.

'Is that why you told him to buy his house and give it to you?'

My raised voice bounced off the rafters in the building and echoed through the room.

He shook his head. 'You're still misjudging me, Frank. But that's okay. I know things have been difficult for you since you were forced out of the police. I spoke to your father about using an equity-release scheme so he could have a bit of money to enjoy himself in - and I don't want to offend you here - the twilight of his years.'

'Equity release?'

In a split second, he'd transformed himself from a self-less man of the people into a financial advisor.

'It's a way to unlock the value of your property and turn it into a cash lump sum.'

I didn't need him to explain it to me like a school kid.

'He'd buy the house from Andreas Housing, then sign it over to you to pay off his debt and also receive some money – is that right?'

He nodded. 'Plus, he'd continue to live there until he... well, until he died. My company has done this with many residents in the town.'

I pulled up a box and sat on it.

'Jesus, Tony. How do you sleep at night with all these good deeds sweeping through your veins?'

He grabbed his jacket from the chair and slipped it on.

'I can't lie to you, Frank; I am involved in some things which aren't lawful.'

'You mean like running illegal gambling dens in the back rooms of pubs?'

'There's a lot more to it than that. Do you want to see some of it?'

Now I was turning into Alice, and he was the Mad Hatter. 'Lead the way.'

The Goth girl joined him, but his gang of goons stayed well away. If he continued to play the man of the people role, I might get the old man's gambling debts written off. They walked to the end of the room and through another door.

'I hope you're not afraid of going underground, Frank.'

I shrugged. 'It's one of my favourite Jam songs.'

The Goth girl gave me a confused look as she led us down a set of stairs. Tony spoke to me as we descended.

'Didn't you have a romantic interlude with Shelley Speck in the basement of this pub?'

How did he know that? Did Shelley tell him?

'That was a long time ago.'

The Goth girl made a choking sound with her throat. I thought she was ill until I realised she was taking the piss out of me. Then we reached the bottom, and she removed a key from the black leather bag around her waist. She used it to open the door ahead of us. He pressed a switch and lights flickered on like an airport runway.

My jaw dropped. 'This isn't the basement I remember.'

It was huge, far bigger than the two rooms above us. It stank of blood and sweat. Tony put his arm on my shoulder.

'I purchased the pub when the brewery went out of business. I had no intention of reopening it as a public house again. There's no money in that, and I had grander plans for it.' He waved his arms around like the ringmaster at a carnival. 'It took a while to get the supports for the roof in and knock through the existing walls, but it was all worth it in the end, don't you think?'

I moved into the middle of the concrete floor, peering down at the familiar stains of dried blood.

'What is this place, Tony?'

It was the Goth girl who answered.

'It's where you'll fight for your life, Walker.'

20 STREET FIGHTING MAN

'You want me to take part in a fight club?'

I'd always perceived myself as a Brad Pitt looka-like, but the reality was different.

The Goth girl told me her name was Lydia before adding to my confusion.

'Don't be stupid, Walker.' The sneer matched the daggers in her jaded green eyes. 'You're going to be our great pretender, the champion to unite all the estates under Thompson rule.'

She sounded like a proud parent. Was she related to Toenail?

'Kid, you're making my bruises hurt.'

Lydia was another one who enjoyed the sound of her voice.

'Supermarket trolleys with wonky wheels have made less hapless journeys than you to get here, Walker. You're an inspiration to idiots everywhere.'

She appeared to be enjoying herself while Thompson stood back and left her to it. Lydia may have only been a teenager, but I wouldn't let her have it easy.

'Better people have called me worse things. Are you Tony's charm advisor?'

Her purple lips shimmered into a darker shade.

'You're a joke without a punchline, Walker; someone so stupid they don't even realise why they're here.'

I turned to the organ grinder. 'Are you going to put me out of my misery, Tony, or do I have to go ten rounds with one of your sluggers?'

I might have preferred that to this verbal banter with Lydia the Goth.

'Follow me, Frank, and all will be revealed.'

Thompson walked to the back of the room, the stink of bleach and ammonia wafting from the shadows. I strode behind him, thankful my teenage antagonist didn't join us. When we reached the end, he pointed to something on the wall. I moved closer to get a better look, seeing a map of the town.

'My mother used to have one of these in the house, rolled up and kept in the cupboard. I think they were printed in the 1970s.'

She'd roll it onto the dining room table and show me where we were in the grand scheme of things on the Parish Hills estate. Now, looking at Thompson's eager eyes, I guessed he wanted to teach me a lesson.

'It was the same in our house, but my father, a rabid member of the Socialist Party, used it to educate me on local history.' He placed his finger on the edge of the map. 'This town began here two hundred years ago as a small farm in an agriculture-driven country coming to terms with the industrial revolution. The discovery of iron and steel soon transformed the area into the bedrock upon which Victorian Britain strode across the globe. People flooded here searching for jobs in these new industries, but where could you put them?'

'You build an infrastructure.'

He ran his palm over the map.

'Indeed, which is why we have a dozen estates built for the workers and their families, plus three more which grew out of the bigger farms transformed into communities for the landed elite and what was to become the middle classes.'

'Is this connected to you wanting to buy my old man's house? Is it the speech you give to people when describing your burgeoning property empire?'

'History connects us all, Frank.' He moved to the side and tapped the map where both of us grew up. 'The point I'm trying to make is that the town is always evolving, constantly changing, and you're about to play a significant part in the next development.'

Those bruises on the back of my neck hummed against my spine.

'That sounds great, Tony. How am I going to do that?'

He reached into his pocket and removed bits of paper. I didn't have to look too hard to see my father's scrawled signature on them.

'Here, these are yours.' He held them towards me.

'What's the catch?'

I didn't take them, my mind working overtime and imagining he'd sprayed Russian poison all over them, which wouldn't make any sense since they were in his hand.

'*Quid pro quo*, Frank. You get these if you give me what I want.'

Now we were getting to the nitty-gritty, with no vague teenage Goth talk to confuse me.

'What do you want?'

He walked away from the map and pointed to the middle of the room.

'You weren't far wrong when you mentioned this space being used for a fight club.' His lips curled upwards like drunken slugs. 'But it's something more important than that.'

'You want me to be one of your fighters?'

The hammering at the back of my skull was increasing.

He pushed the gambling debts closer to me.

'You'll be more than just a fighter; you'll be competing for the unofficial title of King of this town.'

At first, I thought he was messing with me, taking the piss to get me off guard before his goons piled in and beat the crap out of me. But now, peering into his face, I saw how serious he was.

'This has something to do with your criminal empire, doesn't it?'

His eyes narrowed, went rigid and cold. 'There's no need to insult me, old friend.' He put the papers into his pocket. 'If you don't want to comply, I'll send someone to speak to your father tomorrow.'

I let out a deep sigh. 'Just tell me what you want, Thompson.'

'I told you the other day these communities have given up on official organisations pretending they're looking out for them, turning to more reliable local options.'

The image of the food boxes in the other room returned to me. 'I remember.'

He glanced back at the map. 'Well, we may be a small town compared to most of the country, but it still takes a group of people to oversee all the different communities. Moreover, these positions of authority are not randomly handed out or voted on in elections; we have ways of deciding something of such importance.'

'Let me guess. You have your version of gang wars to decide who will become modern feudal lords.'

He shook his head. 'That would be far too violent and cause untold collateral damage, not to mention how it would attract the attention of the authorities. So no, we came up with a wiser solution: each community nominates a champion to fight for them and, sometimes, to fight for control over the other communities.'

I placed my hand on my heart, trying to stop it from cracking with laughter.

'You want me to be your champion, to fight in some warped contest so that you can increase your criminal control in the town?'

'You'll need some warm-up fights first to get you ready for the bout against the Russian.' He looked at me like a farmer scrutinising a cow before sending it off to the slaughterhouse. 'You're still a big man, Frank, but I see you're out of shape. Leaving the coppers has made you lazy, and returning to a northern diet of fish and chips, curries, and pizzas hasn't done you any favours. But with Lydia's help and your police training, not to mention all those dirty street fighting tricks you used as a kid, I'm confident you'll do our estate and me proud on the big night.'

I couldn't hold it in anymore and burst out laughing. It must have been in there a long time, hibernating from before I left London, and tumbled out of me like an alcoholic hyena in a brewery.

'I always knew you were dumb, Tony, and God knows how you gained this little empire of yours, but that's one of the stupidest plans I've ever heard, and I've sat through talks by several Home Secretaries and their latest ideas for fighting crime.'

I bent over and coughed on the floor. When I snapped my head up, Lydia had re-joined us.

'Shall I send a crew round to his house for the old man?'

My joy disappeared in an instant as I glared at her.

'I need to consider it, Tony. While I'm doing that, you have to do something for me as a gesture of good faith.'

'You can have the slips, Frank. I trust you with them.'

All that meant was they didn't matter to him. He'd punish my father whether or not I went along with his mad scheme. But I needed time to think my way out of it.

And I needed something else.

'I want you to find Harpo for me, Tony. With your resources and contacts, you must have someone who knows or who has seen our curly red-haired strangler.'

He rubbed at the stubble on his chin. 'You're in no position to bargain with me, Frank.'

'Maybe not, but it's the only way I'll consider doing your dirty work.'

Lydia grinned at me. 'You don't need him, Tony. You know what I'm capable of.'

Jesus, she was some kind of ninja assassin and a spooky sadist. And I thought London was full of weirdos.

He ignored her and came to me.

'Even with all my resources, there's no guarantee I'll find anything about this mystery man of yours.'

'Grace saw him in the pub, so someone else must have.'

'The police are searching for him.'

I rolled my eyes. 'You've already told me how much better you and your organisation are than them, so now's your chance to prove it.'

He pondered my words for a second, but I knew his ego

wouldn't allow him to miss an opportunity to show me his prowess.

'I want you back here at eight tomorrow night for your first training session, Frank. I'll tell you if I've discovered anything then.'

It was my turn to do the pondering, but it didn't take long: what choice did I have? I could leave the search for Harpo to the police, but I had to deal with Thompson at some point.

'What type of training?'

He glanced at the Goth girl. 'That's down to Lydia. But we don't have time to get your weight down or increase your fitness, so she'll have to weave her magic on you.'

I didn't know whether to laugh or cry. I stared at Lydia.

'How old are you, kid?'

She reached into her pocket, removed a piece of chewing gum, and popped it into her mouth.

'I'm old enough, pops.'

I sucked air into my lungs and gazed at this strange duo. I had fewer than twenty-four hours to figure something out.

But there was another thing on my mind.

'Do you know what happened to Dolores Cook?'

'I thought you had something to do with that, Frank.'

He was trying to wind me up again. However, two could play at that game.

'She disappeared on an estate you control.'

'I'm not God. I don't have eyes and ears everywhere. Plus, of the few CCTV cameras in the town, most of them don't work.'

'But you can ask around about her, for me?'

Lydia stood on her tiptoes and whispered to him. Then she blew a pink bubble at me. It popped, and she sucked the gum back into her mouth.

'Lydia thinks you must be smitten by your missing neighbour, Frank. But, of course, that can't be true, can it? I mean, you're about fifteen years older than her.'

Lydia's shoulders shivered as she kept on chewing.

'I'm concerned for her safety, as you should be.'

He threw his hands into the air. 'I'm sure she'll turn up at some point. So, do we have a deal?'

He held out his hand. I refused it and strode away.

'I'll give you my answer tomorrow, Thompson.'

I left the same way I come in, past those boxes for the food banks and outside into the night. I looked upwards, not expecting to see any stars since the town was still riddled with the smog accumulated over the years.

My fingers found the bruises again, the result of the last fight I was in; only it wasn't much of a fight and more of an ambush. I stepped through the hole in the fence and headed home.

Now I had to come up with my own ambush.

21 GLORY DAYS

It was late when I got back, with the old man tucked up in bed. I followed his example and slept until ten. When I'd washed the night's excitement out of my eyes, I went downstairs to find him in the dining room. He'd made himself a large sandwich and was munching on it.

My appetite was lacking, but I checked the fridge and the cupboards in the kitchen, seeing they were nearly empty. It was a good sign he was eating when I wasn't there. Today's *Daily Mirror* was on the table in front of him with a magnifying glass in the middle of the paper. He couldn't read without it now.

I pointed at the newspaper. 'Where did you get that from?'

'Harry popped it through the door this morning.' That was the neighbour who wasn't dead or missing. 'He lets me have it when he's finished with it.'

I'd forgotten about that. Two weeks into my return, I'd come down to see my father in the back garden burning a copy of the *Daily Mail*. I told him off for doing something so dangerous, but decided he was doing a service to the community, if not the rest of the world. I put the kettle on and asked if he wanted a cup of tea.

'Only if you drop a nip of brandy in it.'

I wasn't sure we had any spirits in the house, but I wouldn't have done it if we had. There was no point having him tipsy this early in the day, especially since I was going out again. So I plopped myself in the chair opposite him.

'I have to go out soon, and I'll restock at the shops. Will you be okay for a bit? I wasn't happy with you on your own here last night.'

He picked up the magnifying glass and stared at a story about a fish and chip shop selling battered chocolates. I guessed those culinary delights were available only in Scotland.

'I wasn't on my own. Mary came to see me. She was hungry, so I gave her some food. We had a natter about you.'

The kettle screamed as I considered his words.

'Mary? My sister, Mary?'

'Of course. Who else would I mean?' He lifted the magnifying glass and peered at me through it, one giant eye scrutinising me. 'I hadn't seen her for such a long time, but the others always visit when you're not here.'

'The others?' I didn't like where this was going.

'Thomas and Colleen. They didn't leave me for years like you did.'

I didn't know how to answer that, so I retreated into the kitchen to make some tea. I wanted some of that brandy as well, but I dumped three sugars into the dark liquid and returned to the table. He'd moved on to another story, about a bloke having a flesh-eating tapeworm pulled from his brain.

'What do you talk about?' The cup was warm against my hands.

He put the magnifying glass down. 'What do you think they talk to an old man about? They tell me about their lives and what they're doing.'

The weariness in his eyes made me tired. The increasing lines crisscrossing his face obscured most of his flesh. Was it a good idea to continue with this, to encourage him in his fantasies? Would it do more harm than good?

'What was Colleen saying?'

He grinned at me. 'She's retired now, living in Spain with that fool she married.'

I nodded at him. The last time I'd checked Colleen's Facebook page, she was divorced and living in Cornwall.

'What about Tommy?'

His smile disappeared. 'Your brother's name is Thomas. He hates the army.'

I shook my head. 'He should have listened to you, Dad – you told him not to join.'

He waved a finger at me. 'You know I'm always right, son.'

'You talked to Mary about me last night when I was out?'

He bit into the other half of his sandwich, cheese dripping over the paper before he scooped it up through cracked fingernails.

'She wanted to know what you were doing, so I told her about Thompson. She doesn't like him.'

I wasn't sure how many people liked Tony Thompson, but he appeared to have gained several loyal and peculiar hangers-on. The old man finished his sarnie, and I drank most of my tea. I didn't have the heart to tell him his conversations with his older daughter and the others were all in his mind. And did it matter in the end? They were all real to him. They meant more to him now, in the twilight of his years, than at any time he'd spent with his children when they were younger. Maybe fake memories were of equal importance to genuine ones.

The chair squeaked as I stood. He'd returned to his newspaper and magnifying glass, studying a story about a YouTube influencer who quit her job to eat food in front of the cameras for her thousands of subscribers. I wondered what he'd make of that. We had a running joke about social media influencers in London, calling them Influenzas. They appeared to have infested most of the modern world with, as far as I could see, no apparent benefits to the rest of civil-isation.

He flicked through the paper as I left him to it. I made sure the door was locked when I left, contemplating what imaginary conversations the old man would have this day.

I walked through the town to the police station. This place used to be the dirt under my nails and the film of industrial breath settling on my skin. I'd found it stifling then, a construction pressing down on me so I couldn't breathe anymore; that was why I'd had to get out. Now, it was nothing more than somewhere I had to endure until I decided where to go next.

After weaving through a labyrinth of roads and dodging any unwanted curious gazes, I emerged under the train lines, the station ahead of me. A group of women were outside the building, maybe a dozen of them, carrying plac-ards claiming JUSTICE FOR REFUGEES. Two officers made sure they didn't infringe too much on police property.

I was about to give them a wide berth – not because I didn't sympathise with their sentiment, but because I didn't want to get bogged down with anything else as I had prob-lems of my own to sort out – when I heard someone mention finding the missing.

My curiosity took me left, where I was stopped by a stern-looking woman staring at me.

'Can I help you?'

Her accent was local, that northern twang most southerners thought was Geordie, but wasn't. I remembered my manners and held my hand out to her.

'Hi; I'm Frank. I was wondering what was going on here.'

I felt the smile extend from my eyes to my mouth, but she didn't appear impressed.

Suspicion filled her face. 'Are you with the police?'

'No, I'm not.' Telling her I was an ex-copper might not have been a good idea. 'I'm here to get information on a missing person, and I overheard what some of your friends said.'

My arm ached, so I dropped my hand.

Her eyes narrowed behind her thick glasses and she twisted her face. It was hard to tell her age; she could have been younger or older than me. She had long snow-white hair like that woman from *Game of Thrones*, tied behind her head. She continued to scrutinise me before the frost melted and her lips curled up. Finally, she opened her jacket to show me an ID badge hanging around her neck.

'I'm Izzy Barnes. I work for the Refugee Service.' She didn't hold out her hand, but her whole demeanour transformed into sweetness and light. Then she gave me a grin that was wider than the horizon. 'You're thinking of Izzy, wizzy, let's get busy, aren't you?'

I wasn't, but I didn't see the need to tell her that.

'Isn't that from *Sooty and Sweep*?'

Sooty was a glove puppet yellow bear created for kids in the 1950s, still going strong seventy years later.

Her shoulders relaxed and her eyes widened, even

though the group of women still protested outside the police station.

'My mother loved the show when she was a kid. So I guess I was lucky not to be Christened Sweep.'

Her smile was so enchanting, I felt guilty about not telling her I was a former detective inspector. Instead, I focused on what she was doing.

'Has someone you know gone missing?'

She nodded. 'Four children haven't been seen for more than a week, each of them from a refugee family.' There was concern and anger in her voice.

'Young kids?'

'All of them are teenagers, fifteen to seventeen-year-olds. The police are classing them as runaways, but I know their parents, these women with me, and they all say their children wouldn't just up and go like that, especially in a new country they know little about.'

'Are they girls?'

I tried not to think of what might have happened to them. Izzy shook her head.

'All are boys.' She paused and bit her lip. 'Though there could be more we – the Refugee Service – aren't aware of. Some of the families are reluctant to come to us about this and won't go anywhere near the authorities in case they're deported.'

I'd seen nothing of this in the news. 'I thought the media would have been all over this.'

She lifted her hands and cracked her knuckles. 'These kids are the wrong colour and speak the wrong language for that. I went to the local paper, but all they're concerned about is this so-called Midnight Strangler and the woman who's disappeared.'

She'd reminded me of why I was there, so I tried to give her something positive to think about.

'I'm on my way to see one of the detectives inside. I'll tell them about this.'

Izzy stuck her hand out as I moved to leave, and there was a card between her fingers.

'Thank you, Frank. Every little helps. This is my mobile number if you learn anything.'

I took it from her and smiled again. It looked like I was collecting cards and new female acquaintances. I left the women to their protest and entered the police station. The person on reception, a woman with the face of a frustrated bulldog, grimaced at me.

'I'm here to see Detective Inspector Rose.'

'Do you have an appointment?'

'Yes,' I lied.

The bulldog flared her nostrils and nodded to a row of seats behind me.

'You can wait there.'

I did as instructed, removing my phone as I sat down. First, I looked online for missing teenagers in the town and got zero results. Next, I searched for the Midnight Strangler, which returned over twelve thousand links, some of which were for a disease of the same name, plus a rave tune.

There was nothing about Harpo in any of the reports, only the usual guff about the police and their ongoing investigation. I'd been involved with most of this before, only from the other side. Where I'd worked, the Major Investigation Team handled everything once a homicide was detailed to them, including dealing with the media. The rule of thumb was to keep them at arm's length unless you thought they might be of some help to the investigation, which was rarely the case.

Therefore, I didn't expect the media to enlighten me in my search for Harpo and Dolores.

The local chatter on Twitter and Facebook was also useless, just loads of people slagging off the victims and making crazy claims about who was to blame, everyone from the postman to the Ghost of Echo Park. That was a new one to me, but my name wasn't mentioned; not yet, at least.

'Is it your turn to visit me, Walker?'

I stood and opened my hands. 'I didn't bring any flowers, DI Rose.'

'Good job too. I hate romantic gestures.'

I followed Rose to her desk and sat down without an invitation.

'Is there any news about Dolores?'

'Why don't you make yourself comfortable, Frank?'

'I thought you'd never ask. So, any leads on my missing neighbour?'

Strange how quickly I'd come to think of her as my neighbour, which meant I perceived my father's house as mine as well. Still, a house isn't a home.

'You expect a lot in less than twenty-four hours, don't you?'

'That's only because I know how good you are, Inspector.'

'Did this flattery routine ever work for you when you were a copper?'

'I nailed a couple of serial killers with it.'

Rose leant into her chair and laughed. 'Touché, Frank; touché.'

She grabbed a pen and did that trick again where she rolled it between her fingers, and I understood how the pen felt.

'I guess you haven't found Harpo, then?'

Rose pursed her lips, and for one second, I thought she was going to blow me a kiss. But, of course, she didn't; it was something so much better than that.

'He's locked up downstairs. Would you like to see him?'

DI Rose took me through the station, past her colleagues, and down to the cells. After getting over the shock of the police having Harpo in custody, the beating of my heart had returned to normal. We strode past the custody sergeant and a detention officer. They acknowledged Rose as we went down, past several empty cells, and towards the last one.

'How did you find him?' I said.

'We got an anonymous call last night about where he was,' Rose said.

'I never liked anonymous calls.'

More often than not, when we discovered who they were from, they ended up being either disgruntled partners or criminal competitors.

'You take what you can get up here.'

She indicated for me to look through the hatch and into the cell. I bent my head and peered through. A rough-looking man was propped up against the far wall, sitting on a bed and asleep. His shock of curly red hair was unmissable.

'Do you recognise him, Frank?'

'No,' I said. 'Apart from the red hair, what's the justification for having him here?'

'We found a pair of gloves on him which match the fibres discovered on George Cross's corpse and Grace Marsh's neck.'

'He was wearing them?' I tried not to sound too excited.

'They were in his pockets. It was enough to bring him in for questioning.'

'You'll ask him about Dolores?'

'Of course we will, Frank, and you'll be the first to know if we get anything from him.'

She moved past me and towards the exit. I peered one more time through the hatch. He looked asleep, but I wondered if he'd heard everything we'd said.

I caught up with Rose as she left the custody suite. 'Where did you find him?'

We talked as we walked. 'He was sleeping rough under the bridge at the end of the river.'

'Do you know who he is?'

She led me back upstairs and to her desk. 'There was no identification on him, which is unsurprising if he's homeless, and I'm waiting for the details on the prints we took. I'd rather not go through the whole teeth and DNA bit if I don't have to, especially as we haven't charged him with anything. And we'll have to arrange his legal representation.'

I slumped into the seat at her desk. She looked surprised I wasn't ready to leave.

'What would you charge him with?'

She glanced at the ceiling, and then back at me. 'We haven't decided yet. I'm waiting on forensics telling me if any of his DNA is inside the gloves.'

'Why would a homeless man do this?'

Rose threw her arms into the air. 'Did your IQ drop when you came home, Frank? Why does anyone do anything, least of all torture and murder?' She didn't wait for me to reply. 'Maybe he stumbled across George outside the park, got into the car, and then strangled him.'

'What about Grace?'

'The back door was open; that's how you entered, so let's say he did the same. Perhaps he wanted food or money or sex or whatever, went upstairs and attacked her.'

'That all seems very convenient. What about George's assertion Harpo paid him and Dolores to set me up?'

'Since George is dead and Dolores is missing, we have nothing to validate the truth of that claim, but even if it's legitimate, who's to say our suspect doesn't have some vendetta against you? Perhaps he has a history with you as a copper. We won't know until we find out who he is.'

She sounded as convinced as I felt. I got up to leave.

'Did you see the group of women protesting outside the station when you arrived?'

Rose puffed out her cheeks. 'I've been here since seven o'clock, Frank. The only things outside were the stink of chemicals and birds searching for food.'

I told her what had happened with Izzy.

'Do you know anything about these missing kids?'

'It's like she said. Social services will treat them as runaways for the first few weeks if they're fifteen and older. We won't get involved unless we have to.' She shrugged. 'It's the way the system works, Frank; you should know that.'

I knew that, but I didn't have to feel good about it. I gave her my thanks and left, worried about what I'd tell Izzy; but I needn't have concerned myself as the group had gone.

My journey home took a detour to the shops to stock up

on provisions. I winced when I swiped my card for the payment, reluctant to check my account since I had to be in the red by now.

The racket from the living room told me where the old man was as I headed to the kitchen to put the shopping away. The clock on the wall indicated I had four hours before returning to Thompson's underground fighting den. I grabbed two cans of cider from the fridge. That would be enough fuel to face whatever that weird Goth girl had in store for me.

I took the booze into the living room, my head flinching from the sonic boom from the TV. He was sitting against the bottom of the chair, legs crossed with the photographs spread across the floor.

Did I want to go down Memory Lane once more?

'I brought you a drink.' I placed it next to him.

'I've got a present for you as well.'

He reached behind him, pulled out a shoebox and handed it to me. I nearly dropped my drink onto the carpet when I saw what was inside it: hundreds of twenty-pound notes.

'What's this?'

'I've been saving my pension.'

The state pension was about seventy quid a week, so there was no way this money could have come from that. Was it from his gambling? Not with Thompson, but somewhere else?

'Are these from winning bets?'

He shook his head as I opened the cider for him.

'I haven't gambled in years. I told you, it's from my work pension.'

That made more sense. He'd retired from his job thirty years ago, so I suppose he could have saved such a large amount, but it was worrying he'd forgotten about the gambling. I dumped the notes next to the photos and spent fifteen minutes counting them: they came to over ten thousand pounds.

I whistled. 'Do you know how much is here?'

'A few hundred quid?'

If I told him the truth, would it worry him?

'There's a bit more than that.'

'There are two boxes more upstairs, under my bed.'

I picked the box up. 'Are they full of twenty-pound notes, like this one was?'

'Twenties and tens, I think.'

The can was at my lips to stop me from swearing; instead, I drank greedily. It was cold and sweet as it slipped down my throat. I resisted the urge to pick up the notes and throw them into the air like an actor in a bad Hollywood movie. If the other boxes were the same, he might have over thirty thousand pounds in this house; more than enough to pay what Thompson claimed was owed to him, not that I believed what he'd said about the old man's gambling debts.

And perhaps it could help me with my money problems?

The thought scrambled from my head as I chastised myself for thinking like that.

I returned the cash to the shoebox and put the lid on. This was a problem – a good problem, but I'd return to it later. Now, I focused on what he'd spread over the floor. This time, what interested me was a yellowing and tattered piece of parchment behind a bunch of photos. The left side was torn away, but the opposite side had an image of a Union Jack on it.

'What's that?' I pointed at it.

His fingers shook as he reached over and lifted the

paper. There was moisture in his eyes as he peered at it before giving it to me.

'It's a Certificate of Thanks I got for taking part in Operation Doomsday in Norway during the war.'

Not once growing up had I heard him talk about what he'd done in the war. Now I held this tattered certificate of one of his achievements.

'Operation Doomsday sounds rather ominous.'

'It wasn't so bad. It was May 1945 and the Germans had just surrendered, but the war wasn't over for me. I was nineteen. My regiment was flown into Norway and tasked with the disarmament and repatriation of the German occupation army.'

His voice trembled as he spoke, but there was something in his face, his aged and wrinkled features, which seemed as if he was a teenager again.

'It must have been a difficult time.'

'We were guarding the docks in Stavanger. The locals gave us a wonderful welcome now the Quislings were gone or imprisoned.'

'Quislings?'

'They were the Norwegians who collaborated with the Germans. The first day I got there, I saw several women with shaved heads because they'd been with German soldiers.'

'Was it dangerous?'

He shrugged. 'All life is dangerous, Frank. You've just got to get on with it.'

The paper was brittle in my hands. I read the front, and then turned it over, seeing numbers written in biro.

'What's this?' I said.

He took the certificate from me, his eyes narrowing as

he peered at the numbers. The memory seemed beyond his grasp until he grimaced and it returned.

'My parents were playing cards and they had no paper to keep the score on.'

My lips parted, my mouth hanging open like a disused bin. As a teenager, he'd risked his life for others, received a certificate of commendation for it, and this was how his mother and father had responded.

I didn't know what to say to him.

He took a drink from the can, staring at it as if he'd never seen such a thing before. He put the certificate back with the photos. Were these memories painful for him? Had he kept them locked in the shadows all these years?

And why were they coming out now?

'I need to get some albums to keep all these mementoes safe,' I said.

He struggled to his feet and slumped into his chair.

'Once the memories have gone, these are all we have left.'

I looked at the pile of photos, sipping on the cider as I gazed at them.

Sometimes, there are memories better forgotten.

Now, I had to concentrate on the present if I wanted us to have a future.

23 TUBTHUMPING

There was no one to greet me when I returned to Thompson's Thunderdome. So I took the same route inside and down the long corridor into the main room. The parcels and the food banks were gone, replaced with a bored-looking fat ginger cat. It glared at me as I walked in.

'Don't worry about him, Fudge. He's no danger to you.' Lydia strode forward. 'He's no danger to anyone.'

She emerged from the shadows, dressed in black, like an ominous wave washing towards me, carrying a silver-tipped cane.

I pointed at the stick. 'Are we going to do a song and dance routine? You'll be Ginger Rogers to my Fred Astaire?'

The cat crept past me and nudged up to her leg.

'I don't know who they are, old man.'

'Maybe I'll teach you something tonight.'

'That seems unlikely.'

She dragged the cane across the floor as she strode away, heading for that other room. The moggy trotted behind her, and I followed suit.

'Is Tony here?' I shouted as she reached the door.

'He's out chasing ghosts for you.'

I went after her. She was already across the other side, standing under the map of the town.

'Does Thompson know Harpo's been caught?' I said.

The cat turned its nose up at me, and Lydia wasn't far from doing the same.

'Do you think a homeless man attacked you and Cross?'

'The police found the killer's gloves on him.'

As soon as the words tumbled from my mouth, I knew I shouldn't have said them.

She rolled her eyes at me. 'And I was told you're a great detective.'

Her insults were warming me up. 'So, you're going to train me to win this competition.'

'It's more than a competition.' She used the cane to point at the map of the town. 'Did Tony explain this to you?'

'You mean the machinations of his criminal empire?'

She pouted at me, her lips a delicate shade of purple.

'Your notions of criminality are narrow and outdated. Define what you mean.'

'It's not that hard, Lydia. A criminal is someone who breaks the law.'

The cat circled her feet and eyed me.

'Once a copper, always a copper. You're thinking with the erroneous part of your brain, Walker. If they passed a law legalising violence against women, would you support it?'

'Of course not.'

'Why not, if it's the law?'

I saw the labyrinth she was leading me down, but there was no way out of it.

'Because some things are inherently wrong.'

'Immoral?'

'You could say that.'

'Is it immoral or criminal to pass a law that increases poverty, or escalates homelessness, or takes benefits from the disabled, or marginalises those with mental health issues? Is it a crime to earn billions but pay no tax? Is it a crime to lie to gain votes or make promises you know won't be kept?'

'I understand. You, Thompson and those like him are doing this out of the goodness of your hearts.'

The laughter exploded from her. 'You were a copper for twenty-five years, and you still believe in goodness?'

With such little effort, she'd annoyed me again.

'Can we get on with whatever this is?'

'We have today and tomorrow to prepare you. Can you handle that?'

'Is this a *Game of Thrones* thing where you'll teach me the fine art of combat?'

'At your age, I'm not sure you can learn anything new. So I'm here to remind you how to survive the fights.'

'Fights?'

She pointed at the map again. The cat jumped on the table, its eyes following the movement of the cane.

'Six wardens oversee fifteen plots. Control fluctuates over time, but the one constant is the competition for the most valuable location, the town centre.' She spoke as if she was leading a business meeting. 'Every three years there's a competition for ownership of the centre. That's what you'll be involved in, and I have to prepare you.'

'I haven't boxed for an age.'

In my earliest days in the force, I won a few bouts and trophies before I got bored with it.

'You won't be boxing, Walker. That's why you're here, for me to teach you how to survive three fights in one night.'

This sounded worse by the minute. 'Why three fights?'

'Six wardens and two guests put forward their champion to win the rights for the town centre for the next three years – eight down to four, then the last two.'

'So tell me, what do these rights entail?'

She picked up the cat and it snuggled in her arms.

'For services rendered, the residents are provided with security, plus educational and employment opportunities.'

'Services rendered is another way of saying the residents pay you.'

Lydia shrugged. 'That's how capitalism works, Walker.'

'What types of security do you provide in this enterprise?'

'All types – somewhere to stay if you're homeless; clothing for those in poverty; food and drink for anyone struggling to pay their bills. We step in when violence and crime touch the lives of innocent people. We provide jobs and educational opportunities.'

'It sounds very altruistic.' She was repeating what Tony had told me yesterday. 'Tell me more about this fighting competition.'

'Eight champions, seven fights before we end up with a winner. Then we all go home.'

'How long are these fights?' I wasn't expecting Queensbury Rules.

'Fifteen minutes each in the first round, then twenty, and thirty in the final. No weapons and no rules. The winner is the last one standing.'

'What happens if both are standing?'

'Then the crowd votes on it.'

'There'll be people watching?'

'They'll be doing more than that. The gambling is as important as the outcome.'

I knew there had to be something else to it.

'Let me guess: Tony will get his share of the betting.'

'The fights won't be here. They'll take place in a neutral venue, but all the wardens receive a percentage. And he'll be betting on you.'

I grinned and shook my head. 'Which other mug did you have set up for this before I came along?'

She dropped the cat to the floor and it hissed at me. Lydia put her fingers into her mouth and whistled long and loud. Footsteps behind me followed it. I turned to see the tallest and biggest of Thompson's goons approaching.

He didn't look happy.

'Walker, this is Chuck. You'll be taking his place in the competition.'

He didn't offer to shake my hand. Instead, I returned my focus to her.

'He can still compete if he wants. I'm not fussy.'

'I'd prefer another alternative, but you must have done something in that pub to impress Tony.'

Perhaps he didn't care about the money or the power, wanting to see me beaten to a pulp and humiliated in front of the locals.

'Am I supposed to fight him now?'

I pointed at Chuck. The man grinned at me through a toothless mouth. It was unnerving. Lydia strode past us and into the middle of the floor. The cat and Chuck followed her. I stopped and watched them.

'Take your jacket off, Walker, and hand it to me.' I did as instructed. 'There's nothing on the feet or hands when you fight, so get the shoes off as well. I'd recommend wearing a short-sleeved shirt and shorts for better movement. Or you can go shirtless to show off your physique.' She looked me up and down, top to bottom, and then back again. 'You're a big man, but that'll only get you so far. If you can avoid the Russian until the final, you might have a chance.'

She seemed angry with me and I didn't know why. I removed my shoes.

'This sounds like one of those terrible Sylvester Stallone *Rocky* movies.'

Chuck scowled at me. Lydia was now amused.

'That's before my time, Walker.'

Before I could reply, she swung the cane at me. Most people would have lifted their arm to block the attack, but I stepped away so it missed me. She pulled the cane back to her side. Chuck snorted derision at me. Lydia's expression was different, with a glint in her eye and a slight curve in her mouth. Now she appeared pleased.

'Tony might have been right about you, Walker. Maybe you will have a chance.'

Chuck broadcast his disapproval. 'He's got no chance if he's running away.'

Lydia rolled her eyes at him before addressing me.

'Ignore him. He's pissed off because you're taking his place. But he'd never stand a chance in this competition.'

Chuck wasn't about to take the insult, thrusting his fist at me. 'I'd whip his arse in a heartbeat.'

She went to him and put her hand on his arm.

'You'll get your opportunity tomorrow.' There was more tenderness in her voice than I'd heard from her before. She must have guessed what I was thinking. 'Don't get the wrong idea, Walker. Chuck's far too dumb and not my type.'

He didn't appear upset by those insults. I stared at her.

'Is this part of the training?'

She tapped the side of her head. 'For you to win, you'll need to use this as much as your physique. Tony tells me you were always the cleverest in their group. Is that true?'

It was time to stick my chest out.

'You don't get to be a detective inspector without having some brains.'

'Let's test that.'

Lydia moved, swinging down at me with the cane. I wasn't as quick as her, but speedy enough, moving back as she kept swinging. Then she stopped aiming for my head and went for the legs. I expected it and kicked up, catching the wood and forcing her away as the stick cracked against the bone in my foot. I hopped to one side and grimaced.

Chuck laughed. 'He's useless. Tony must be mad to trust him.'

Lydia didn't hesitate. She made the same moves against him as she'd done with me. The cane came down high towards his head and he blocked it with his arm. Recent experience had taught me it was heavier than it looked. He pulled his arm down and cried out. Then, for good measure, she kicked him in the stomach. He tumbled to the ground and the cat jumped out of the way. I nursed my bruised foot as she stood over him.

'He's already lasted longer than you, Chuck. Do you still want to question Tony's decision?'

He whimpered as he lay there. 'No.'

She turned to me. 'Are you ready to start?'

'We haven't started?'

'What does the pain in your toes tell you?'

'Kick nothing.'

Her lips curled up and I would have sworn it was a genuine smile.

'Not with the top of your foot. Don't use your feet for attack unless you have to, and then only use the bottom like this.'

She lunged at Chuck with her foot aimed at his head, but she stopped a couple of inches away. He let out a massive sigh as Lydia put her leg down.

'If this Russian is the toughest of the bunch, what happens if I get drawn against him in the first round?'

'It won't happen. Tony will make sure of that.'

'Okay. So how do I survive three rounds of brutality?'

'By making sure it's not brutal. If you punch without gloves, your hands will be damaged; your knuckles will swell, so you can't use them. It'll be the same for your feet. Every fight is the same: it's more brawn than brain. The lugs come in, all muscles and sweat, and try to beat each other's brains out. It ends up being the survival of the fittest. You're big and beefy, but old and out of condition. So you have to outlast your opponents.'

'Thanks for the compliments, but that's easier said than done.'

'Hit like this.' She thrust her arm out with a hand in the air. 'But at some point, you'll need to put your opponent on the floor. Then, you'll have to punch, doing the most damage to them and the least harm to you. Which means you hit them where?'

'In the throat.' I'd learnt this lesson at thirteen. 'If I've got this right, you want me to dodge, block, and then strike the throat?'

'It will be the best way for you to win.' She glanced at

the cat, and it ran to her. 'Tomorrow, you'll practise with Chuck and we'll see how ready you are.'

She picked up the moggy and stepped over Chuck as he lay on the floor.

I watched them leave and wondered how my life had come to this.

The next day started with two phone calls. The first was the old man's test results from the doctors. The woman didn't want to give me them initially, but she relented when I pointed out he couldn't get to the surgery.

'It appears your father is showing symptoms of the early stages of dementia,' she told me as if she was reading out a train timetable. When I asked her what to do next, she gave me the social services' phone number to get him an interview with a caseworker. What would happen after that was anyone's guess.

The second call wasn't as miserable, but it didn't put me in a good mood either. I don't know how Rose had acquired my mobile number, but she had.

'You're a hard man to contact, Walker.' She sounded a lot happier than I felt.

'Have you got positive news for me?'

'I'm afraid not. Our mystery bloke is still a mystery. We asked around some spots where he's been sleeping rough, but people were reluctant to talk to us. The only info they provided was that he could be an ex-squaddie who might have done tours in Iraq and Afghanistan.'

'Hasn't he spoken?'

'That's the other thing. He can't speak because his vocal cords were sliced at some point. There's a scar on his neck we only discovered once he was cleaned up.'

'Harpo can't talk?'

'Indeed. Perhaps that's why he got the name.'

'Can he write or use a digital device?'

'If he can, he hasn't so far. However, it looks like he might have some mental health issues, so he's been transferred to the psych ward at the hospital. We've put a guard on his room.'

'Have you kept one for Grace?'

'For now, but if we decide this guy's our perpetrator, we'll move her to another facility. There's no change in her condition.'

'What about the gloves you found on him? Are they enough to charge him with anything?'

'His DNA is on them, same for our two victims, but we might not charge him if the specialists say he's not fit to stand trial.'

'Then what?'

I imagined Rose shrugging at the other end of the line.

'He'll go to a secure unit.'

It wasn't great, but it was enough for now. Without a name for him, I wouldn't know why he'd tried to stitch me up.

'Any news on Dolores?'

'Nada.'

It was seventy-two hours since she'd gone missing. Unless somebody offered new information, it was unlikely the police would find her. I could only hope she'd decided to disappear and hadn't been snatched by someone.

I considered telling Rose about my upcoming entrance into the illegal bare-knuckle fighting game. It was on the tip of my tongue, but either it fell off or I swallowed it, because I said something else instead.

'I'll ask around on the estate about Dolores. The locals may be more forthcoming with me than your lot.'

'Good luck with that.'

'Thanks. I have a query for you, DI Rose.'

'Fire away.'

'How do Tony Thompson and his brethren get their little fiefdoms to work?'

Her breathing was heavy down the line. 'That's a large question, Walker.' Did she think I was having a go at her and her colleagues? 'Why do you need to know?'

Now I had the perfect chance to tell her about my forthcoming role in Thompson's fight club. But I didn't. I lied instead.

'It might help me find Dolores.'

'It's not your job to find her; that's ours.'

'So you won't tell me about Thompson?'

Her sigh was loud enough to travel down the connection and grip me by the throat.

'It's all about drugs. Everything else, the charity work around the town, is just a front for it.'

'He told me he wasn't involved in drugs.'

She must have put her hand over the phone, but I still heard laughing at the other end.

'And you believed that?'

'Well, I've had a knock on the head.'

'Okay, I'll forgive you that one. Thompson and the others only deal in soft drugs in the town. They know the police won't bring in users, so they keep their production, storage, and distribution hidden from us.'

'There's no hard stuff involved?'

'Not in this town, but they traffic in neighbouring towns and cities.'

'Do they involve kids in this?'

'Not that we're aware of. Why do you ask?'

While in London, I'd investigated county lines gangs, those groups where criminals groomed and manipulated children into drug dealing. The "lines" referred to mobile phones used to control a young person delivering drugs, often to towns outside their home county.

'I was thinking those missing teenage refugee boys might have been dragged into a county lines racket.'

She again put her hand over the phone and spoke to someone near her. Then she got back to me.

'It's worth considering, but the only people we've arrested are small fry, and they never spill the beans.'

Her use of food comparisons made me hungry, but I ignored the ache in my guts.

'What happens with the money?'

'That's the thing; we don't know. If we could track where it goes, we'd have a chance of nailing Thompson. And if we got him, it might lead to others.'

'If I find anything, I'll tell you. Thanks for the info.'

'You're welcome.'

Then she hung up on me.

The old man had his magnifying glass up to a Jack Higgins novel when I entered the living room. An aroma of burnt toast lingered in the air and I guessed he'd had his breakfast. I went into the kitchen and made some for myself. I checked the fridge. A packet of sandwiches was gone, but there was one left. I wouldn't eat much today, not if I would be practising my fisticuffs tonight.

I smiled to myself, but not at the thought of the fighting. My wife always had a problem pronouncing fisticuffs and called it fifty cuffs. I allowed the memory to warm my heart for a minute before stepping into the back room. I opened the drawer where I'd left the spare key for the Cooks' – to search for Dolores, that would be the best place to start.

I removed the key and slipped out the door. I climbed over the fence without caring if anyone saw me. I was inside the house in less than a minute, upstairs thirty seconds later, and it was still a tip. I searched the bedrooms, ignoring the smell of mouse shit and the lack of cleaning.

My feet stuck to the carpet as I went.

The first bedroom had clothes everywhere and the same stink as the rest of the house. I checked the drawers and the cupboard, finding empty fag packets, boxes of matches and a few old photos of Dolores and George. I picked one up, seeing them grinning into the camera as the sea rose behind them. It looked like the spot near the beach where I'd met her a few days ago.

I returned it and checked the other bedroom, only getting the same results and dirty hands, before trudging downstairs and into the living room. The sofa was different from last time. Somebody had taken a knife to it, slicing through the fabric so the furniture had coughed up most of its guts over the carpet.

I kicked the debris away. Nothing was under it, making this look like a wasted trip.

Then I heard the blow coming before I saw it. I ducked to my side, swivelling to bring my fist round and into the soft flesh of his belly. The force of it took him back and down into the sofa's spewed innards. His head thumped into the edge of the furniture and his eyes glazed over. It was the second time I'd seen him like this in fewer than twenty-four hours.

'Stay down, Chuck.' I was ready to hit him again if he didn't.

Had he followed me in here? Was this part of Lydia's training?

'You haven't lost it, Frank. Maybe Lydia was right about you.'

Tony stood behind me, his shoulder resting against the side of the doorway.

I watched Chuck while I spoke to Tony.

'Why are you here?'

'Why wouldn't I be? This is one of my properties.' He glanced around the room. 'I haven't visited since the Cooks moved in, and it seems as if Dolores won't be returning soon. I've lost a tenant and a barmaid, so I'll need to have this place cleaned up before moving new people in.' He pointed at Chuck. 'Are you going to let him up? I understand he has another meeting on the agenda with you tonight, though by the looks of it, it'll be over quick.'

'He can get up,' I said.

Thompson grinned at me. 'Good – as long as you're ready to win for me tomorrow. Remember, your father's debts depend on you succeeding.'

'What? You said I only had to fight for you to erase what he owes.'

'Don't be silly, Frank. You could hit the floor in the first two minutes if that were the case. You need to win all three bouts, so I'm giving you some incentive.'

I stopped myself from lunging at him. Chuck got up and staggered to his side.

'More fool me for trusting you.'

'I trust you as much as you trust me. If it weren't for Lydia, I'd have broken your legs by now.'

I controlled my beating heart. 'She's young for you, Tony, don't you think?'

'Don't be disgusting, Frank. Lydia is family.'

I nearly fell over when he said that. 'She's your kid?'

A veil of sadness consumed him. 'She might as well be, but no, she's not my daughter.' I could've sworn there was a tear in his stony eyes. 'Don't you recollect my younger sister, Ruby?'

It was hard not to. She was six years younger than us, all gangly arms and elbows. An awkward girl with a permanent smile, always smelling of strawberries.

'Sure, Tony, I remember her. She was the total opposite of you, decent and kind.'

'Indeed.' He ignored the insult. 'She got cancer when Lydia was five and died two years later. I've looked after Lydia ever since, though she'd tell you she looks after me.' He wiped at his eyes. 'She's my right hand.'

'That's swell, Tony, bringing a kid up like that. You must be the parent of the year.' I strode forward and pushed past him, my elbow digging into his arm. I was halfway down the hall when I turned to face him. 'How many houses do you own?'

He rubbed at his mouth and considered the question.

'Too many to mention; all but one on this street.'

I left the house, climbed over the fence and returned to the only home Tony Thompson wasn't the landlord of.

25 COMBAT ROCK

It was eight hours later when I faced Chuck again. It was cold in the god-forsaken pub's extended basement, with me standing in a t-shirt and those long shorts Rafa Nadal made fashionable at his peak. Chuck glared and cracked his knuckles, but it wasn't him who interested me.

'You look like a decrepit pirate.' Lydia was next to a table, on which were seven photographs.

'Are these my suitors?'

The cat was missing, but she had her trusty cane and was dressed as if she was about to go jogging.

'If you're lucky, Walker, you'll get to spend an hour grappling with three sweaty men.'

'That's marvellous; who's up first?'

'There's been a change of plan regarding the match-ups. There'll be a blind draw tomorrow before the competition starts, so it'll be a free for all.'

'So, I might get the Russian first?'

'It's a possibility.'

I examined the photos, staring at a group of men who'd

never be described as handsome, just a collection of out-of-shape noses, cauliflower ears, and snarling eyes.

'Which one is he?'

Lydia handed me a photo. He had a muscular physique, numerous tattoos, and scars across his face, with a football-shaped bald head lined with veins.

'His real name is Anatoly, but everyone calls him the Russian.'

I put it back with the others. 'I see imagination is still in short supply around here.' I concentrated on another image of a man with huge biceps as if from a *Popeye* cartoon. 'Who's this?'

Lydia grinned. 'That's Toppo; he's my favourite. He injects his muscles with Synthol to get his arms like that. A lot of bodybuilders do the same.'

'Is it legal?'

'I don't know, but it's allowed in the competition. These men regularly fight here and around the country. It's a lucrative business for some.'

'I bet it is.' For Thompson and his cronies, at least. I glanced at Chuck. 'When do we start?'

She laughed. 'Not with him, yet. He's still smarting from what you did this morning.'

'You heard about that?'

'I hear about everything.' She twirled the cane in her hand.

'What do you know about Dolores's disappearance?'

Lydia shook her head. 'No one knows where she is. It's as if aliens have snatched her away.'

'Okay, but what about kids vanishing from the town?'

She stopped moving. 'What are you talking about?'

'At least four teenage refugee boys have disappeared; their families are distraught. Doesn't Tony, or these other so-called wardens, know anything about this? How can you claim to be in control around here and not know what's happening underneath your noses?'

Chuck got involved in the conversation.

'Nobody cares about those people.' His face was all red as if an overcooked gammon had replaced his skin. 'We have to look after our own first.'

Lydia scowled at him. 'Get the twins.'

She removed a small clock from her pocket as he left, one of those you see chess players use in competition. She plopped it in the middle of the photos.

'You didn't know about the missing kids?'

She ignored the question and pointed the cane at me.

'You need to avoid my attacks for fifteen minutes with no retaliation; do you understand?'

I nodded as she started the timer – then she struck at me. I dodged to the back and the side, again and again. Sometimes I had to use my hands and arms to block the cane before it came for my head. On it went as the time ticked away, our dance under the moonlight filtering through the broken windows in the skylight.

As Chuck and the twins arrived, the clock stopped, and so did she. Sweat covered me, my heart beating faster than a runaway train. Everywhere ached, my hands red raw from where she'd hit me. I wiped at my forehead.

'I need a drink.'

'You've got one minute to recover.' She turned to the others. 'Bob, Terry, you're up.'

They strode over, bull-headed doppelgängers who had my suffering imprinted on their faces.

I spat on the floor. 'Are you trying to kill me, Lydia?'

'If you can't survive this, Walker, you'll have no chance tomorrow.'

I bent over and clutched at my stomach. 'Brilliant.'

She addressed the twins. 'Get either side of him and do what I told you earlier.' Then she turned to me. 'They won't attack together; first one, then the other. So you need to switch between them and block.'

Spittle dripped from my lips. 'I can't fight back?'

'You can, but you have to choose wisely. Once you do, they're allowed to hit you simultaneously. Do you understand?'

I nodded. What I understood was she was a sadist. As that thought lingered in my brain, Bob threw a fist at my head. I slipped backwards, right into Terry punching me in my side. Perhaps it was the other way round, but the pain surging through me was what mattered. My reflex was to move away, back into Bob's reach, but I shifted sideways instead. A second later, they stepped over to sandwich me again.

There were five yards of space between them and me. If I hadn't been so tired from my fifteen-minute exertion with Lydia, I might have had the energy to take them on together. But I could also have collapsed to the floor and given up. It was tempting, but the look of pity on Lydia's face made me more determined to prove her wrong.

Bob threw another punch my way. I didn't move this time, blocking his knuckles with my arm. It hurt like hell, but it must have been worse for him since he grabbed hold of his bruised hand and bent over. I figured it gave me enough time to switch to Terry. I ducked from his fist and swivelled underneath his reach. From behind, I snatched his arm, pulling it back and down. The crack of bone reverberated through the building. As he screamed in agony, I lifted my foot, planted it in the middle of his spine and pushed him towards his brother. They hit each other and tumbled to the ground.

I stared at Lydia. 'Are we done?'

She used her cane and pointed behind me. I twisted around, expecting another confrontation, only to see the cat scowling at me. Had she trained the damn beast to attack me? Unfortunately, I was a fraction too late to realise it was a distraction.

'You've had this coming, Walker.'

Chuck punched me in the same spot the twins had. Electric agony swept through me. He hit me two more times on either side of the first punch. I staggered forward, stumbling towards the cat. It sprinted away, spitting as it went. It jumped into Lydia's arms.

'Don't let me down now, Frank.'

I couldn't tell if she was taking the piss or not. The whole of my torso was on fire, with flames of electricity flowing down my legs as they wobbled and I weaved.

'You'll live, Walker, but I'll beat you into a pulp, so Mr Thompson will have to put me back into the contest tomorrow.'

I wanted to say I'd swap places, but the only thing to come out of my mouth was an insult.

'Chucky boy, you'll fold like a cheap suit. I was going to leave you alone, but I'll break both your hands for a laugh.'

Below his wild eyes was a dishevelled grin.

'You're out of practice. Now I'm about to make your suffering last a long time.'

I bent over, clutching at my new wounds, my lungs struggling to find air. I must have looked like a man out on his feet. He stepped at me with his fist held high, ready to thrust it at me like a lightning bolt. But I let go of my guts and pushed my palm into his knuckles. I may have been older than him and winded, but I had more muscle in my arm and legs. I wrapped my hand around his, using my legs to push us towards Lydia and the cat on the table.

We crashed into the middle of it. She dodged out of the way at the last second, the table dropping the moggy on Chuck. It panicked and stuck its claws into his cheeks. He screamed and tore at it as I rolled away from them. I bowled through the fallen photographs, staring at the scene in front of me that looked like something out of a live-action demented *Tom and Jerry* cartoon.

The cat leapt from Chuck, his face littered with scratches and cuts, blood dripping into his eyes and down his cheeks.

'I'm going to kill you, Walker,' he shrieked as I got up.

'Time to finish him, Frank.'

Lydia pointed her cane at the bleeding man. He was disorientated and manic. She was right, though; if I didn't do something now, he'd be a frantic whirl of aggression capable of anything.

Chuck stood and glared at me, wiping the blood from his face. I'd grabbed some photos off the floor with me, and, as he leapt in my direction, I threw them into his blood-stained head. The image of the Russian caught him in his right eye. He was lifting his fingers to push it away when I stepped in.

All it took was a punch into his belly and another into his jaw. He collapsed like a marionette with its strings cut. The cat marched forward, squatted, and pissed on his face, an insult added to an injury he deserved.

Lydia moved towards me. 'You did okay, Frank, but you had help from Fudge, which you won't tomorrow. And you won't be so lucky.'

I wiped the moisture from my mouth. 'Are you Tony's niece?'

Something flashed beneath her calm exterior, a flicker of emotion I hadn't seen before; was it sadness seeping deep into the heart of her?

'He's my uncle, but we're more than just family.'

'And what's that?'

'You could say I'm his apprentice.' She was back to twirling the cane in her hand.

'It's disappointing to see someone so young, somebody with so much potential, become nothing more than a petty criminal.'

A glint of anger crossed her face. 'Once a copper, always a copper.' She planted the cane on the ground. 'What Tony and the others do might break a few of your laws, but we do more good than you'll ever recognise.'

'You can't put yourself above the law, Lydia, no matter what you believe. That will only lead to anarchy and the breakdown of civilised society.'

'I had a teacher like you at school, Walker. He was all about recognising the status quo and not rocking the boat; that was until a drunk driver killed his daughter while she was out riding her bike. He got two months of community service and a few points on his licence for that.'

'That's a terrible tragedy, Lydia, but living outside the law isn't the way anyone should live.'

She laughed like a woman twice her age.

'What's the opposite of a terrible tragedy, a good one?' She walked towards me. 'And anyway, didn't you break some official code to catch a serial killer?'

She was right. What could I say to that?

'What will happen if I don't win?'

'Uncle Tony will be pissed off.' She peered straight into

my face. 'I'd make a better job of it, but you're more skilful than I first thought. You've got a fifty-fifty chance.'

'Thanks.' I grabbed my jacket and bag from the corner. 'What's the arrangement for tomorrow?'

'Be here at six; there'll be a car to take you to the venue.'

'See you then.'

I gave her a mock salute and moved towards the exit. Her voice stopped me in my tracks.

'Is it true what you said, Walker?'

'About what?'

'Those missing kids.'

I guess she didn't know after all.

'The police aren't interested, and neither is the media, but yes, it's true, Lydia.'

She poked her cane at Chuck's sprawled body as I left. Most of me ached like it hadn't in a long time, and that was only after combating a young woman and three idiots.

So how would I survive against the guy with the balloon arms and the Russian?

26 MACK THE KNIFE

The old man was in his best clobber again when I got
back. I ached from my early morning exercise and my
body felt like I was the older person in the room. I waited
for him to ask me where I'd been, but he surprised me with
a different question.

'Since it's the weekend, can we go out?'

He'd been retired for over thirty years, so I assumed
every day was a weekend for him, but I didn't see why not. I
hadn't told him anything about my dealings with Thompson, but I sensed he knew something was going on. Plus, I'd
arranged for a visit from social services on Monday, which I
had yet to inform him about, so who knew when we'd get
the chance to do this again? And I'd never thought I'd look
forward to such a thing.

'Where would you like to go?'

I expected him to nominate a pub, so his answer
surprised me.

'I've never been to McDonald's, so let's try that.'

Sure, why not? At least it would be simple for him to

eat. I didn't know if it was wise to have him near a bunch of Saturday morning kids, but I took him there, anyway.

The taxi dropped us at the corner and I wheeled him towards the building. There were already groups of teenagers hanging around outside and I prepared myself for the usual hostilities, but was surprised when they not only parted the waves to let us through, but one of them opened the door for us. They were better behaved than I was at that age, that's for sure.

I pushed him into a free spot and went to order. There was no point asking him what he wanted because he wouldn't know; it was up to me to make the choices for him now.

The place was heaving, people of all ages shuffling about to get their fast-food treats, my shoes sticking to the floor. The self-service section was the more popular, but I'd read an article once stating there were more germs on those digital screens than a toilet seat. So I went to the counter to speak to a human being and ordered two Big Mac meals.

People came and left as I waited, the hum of voices vibrating around the place. I peered at the old man sitting in the corner, wondering how he'd take a recommendation of moving into a care home if his dementia worsened; or if I dared leave him on his own again. Or was I prepared to stay and look after him, this person I'd lost all feeling for a long time ago?

I rubbed at the bruises under my clothes, staring at the teenagers throwing fries at each other while they played with their mobile phones. Several adults who looked about the same age as me peered at the kids as well, and I assumed they were also thinking about how the world had changed so much since we were that age. I guessed it was progress of a kind. Then I glanced through the window and saw the homeless people huddled against a wall. As a society, we hadn't progressed at all.

There was a pain in my gut that wasn't from hunger. I turned my gaze from those unfortunate folks outside, peering at the grass. A group of seagulls landed on it, and I assumed they were waiting for the patrons of this place to throw them some scraps. Then they moved their legs up and down, a curious dance intended to bring to the surface hidden things. As I observed their toing and froing, a server called my number for our food. I collected it and returned to the old man.

'Mary gave me a message for you.'

I sipped at the Coke and pondered how best to address his ongoing hallucinations. Should I listen to them and keep quiet or try to explain that his oldest kid hadn't spoken to him in fifty years?

'What did she say?'

I unwrapped the burger and handed it to him. It was so large in his hands, he looked like a small child. He took a bite from it and spoke while he chewed.

'She said you should look for the kids.' He picked bits of lettuce from his teeth. 'That's why I wanted to come here.'

I must have appeared as confused as he sounded. 'Why is that?'

He grabbed a fry and crunched on it. 'Because I know there are loads of teenagers at a McDonald's. I've seen it in the adverts.'

He wasn't wrong; the place was full of kids now.

'When did you talk to Mary, Dad?'

He removed a pickle from his burger and dropped it into the tray.

'She always comes at night when you're away, just like Thomas does.'

'Do they come together?'

He gurgled on his Coke, and then wiped his mouth.

'No, those two never liked each other. Thomas won't step into the house. I think the army is still looking for him.'

I didn't tell him I doubted the army would be interested in someone who'd gone AWOL thirty years ago. Instead, I stuck with the easiest thing to say.

'Do you like your junk food?'

He picked bits of meat from the bun, peered at it through watery eyes, and then devoured it. When he'd finished, he replied.

'It's nicer than what we got during the war.'

I couldn't argue with that. This was the second time I'd heard him mention the war. My mother had told me his family were living in virtual poverty when they met, not that hers were much better off, and she thought the war was the best thing that happened to him because he at least got three proper meals a day in the army.

In one of her more outgoing times as a parent, she recounted to me the first time he'd taken her to meet his parents. The house was small, a narrow, one-bedroom outside-toilet place built at the end of the Victorian era. Her fingers had trembled when she spoke about this, remembering how nervous she'd been going there. But the thing which had stuck in her mind the most was when she entered, her future mother-in-law offered her a drink of water, but they were so poor, they couldn't afford any glasses – so she gave it to her in a reused jam jar.

Even during my long time away, that image had never left me, and now here we were, over seventy years after the event, and he was slurping Coke through a paper straw and out of a plastic cup.

'Do you want to go anywhere else?'

I gathered the rubbish on the trays, happy to see he'd eaten all the burger and most of the fries.

'You can take me to the park. I haven't been there in such a long time.'

'Okay, let me dump these first and visit the toilet. Do you need to pee?'

I felt like a parent talking to a small child. He grinned and said no. I emptied the trays and headed upstairs to the toilets. For once, my thoughts were clear of Tony Thompson and his mad schemes, unconcerned about the Cooks and unworried about a red-haired killer called Harpo.

When I came back downstairs, he was gone, wheelchair and all.

My legs froze to the spot, my mind unable to understand what had happened. I scanned the room in a panic, my heart throbbing against my ribs. I stumbled towards where we'd been sitting.

'Excuse me; has anybody seen an old man in a wheelchair?'

I spoke to no one in particular and only received several confused looks in return. In desperation, I peered outside. The dancing birds had gone, but my father was there, next to the grass, speaking to someone who had their head bent down to him. When they raised it, all I saw was the shock of red-haired curls blurring my vision.

I barged past people and was out the door in seconds, my hand reaching for this unknown person. I only stopped at the last instant when I realised it was a woman.

'Is this your dad?' Her voice echoed in my ears and rattled inside my skull.

'Yes, yes it is.'

She raised fingers to her face. 'Oh dear, you look terrified.' She put her hand on my arm. 'I'm sorry to scare you like that. He said he needed to get outside and I didn't see any harm in it.'

Yes, there was no harm in it, apart from the thousand tiny knives jabbing at my insides. I glanced at him as he gazed at the building opposite.

'We lived there when your sisters were born.'

I grabbed the wheelchair and pushed him away, looking at the woman as we left.

'Thanks,' I said without feeling it.

I moved him to the end of the road.

'I'm not crazy, Frank. That building used to be a set of small houses. It was the first house where your mother and I lived. It was long before you were born.'

The wheels came to a shuddering halt as I stopped and glanced behind me. I remembered her telling me once they'd lived here. So he was right, and not in another of his delusional phases.

It was a fifteen-minute walk up the road. I started moving again, past the shops and the shoppers, ignoring the multitude of people out to enjoy their weekend, knowing in a few hours, I'd be doing my best to hammer three strangers into the ground.

When we arrived at the park, I wheeled him through the front and headed for a bench. I slumped onto the fading wood with him next to me, realising I couldn't keep dodging the tough questions forever.

'Do you want to buy the house?'

His neck cricked as he turned to me. 'Are you leaving again?'

The tremble in his voice cut into my heart. I'd left London to hide from my problems. I had few savings, but I could have gone anywhere, yet still, I'd returned to the place I'd never felt loved.

Could I run away once more and leave him to his own devices, a man crawling towards dementia, whose mobility was disappearing, and who owed a local criminal twenty grand in gambling debts?

But he had all that money at home, thousands in shoeboxes.

I placed my hand on his arm. 'No, Dad, not unless you want me to.'

His tears came in floods and it was a struggle to hold mine in. He took my fingers in his and gripped them.

'Now I've got three of you back, and I won't let you leave.'

My goals were simple. I'd win this competition, clear the old man's debts and get him out of Thompson's clutches. Then we could speak to the caseworker from social services on Monday and go from there. Perhaps I could find a part-time job here and settle in like I couldn't before.

We sat there for a while, embracing the silence and the little bit of green inside this dirty old town. Then, for the first time since I'd handed in my badge, I felt alive again.

All I had to do now was survive the rest of the night.

27 FOR WHOM THE BELL TOLLS

When I arrived outside the pub, a car was waiting for me. I didn't recognise the driver, but Chuck was in the passenger seat. I gave him my best smile.

'There's no warm Thompson welcome for me on this auspicious night?'

Chuck scowled at me. 'Get in the back, Walker.'

I did, and they drove off. I had several questions about the night's festivities, but these weren't the people to answer them. I'd left the old man in front of the TV with two cans and a pack of sandwiches. There was no food for me. I was glad he was eating everything I'd bought, but I didn't think it would be a good idea to fill my belly before my forthcoming fisticuffs.

'Where are we going, lads?'

They ignored me. I got my phone and considered sending Rose a message. Before I could, Chuck snatched it from me.

'No phones allowed inside tonight.'

I resisted the urge to grab him by the scruff of the neck

and drag him into the back. I needed to save all my energy and anger for my upcoming challenges.

We exited the estate as the day succumbed to the night, the neon lights of the pubs and takeaways flashing by as we headed into the heart of the town. When the car took a left and then a right, I had a good idea of where we were heading.

'You're going to the sports centre.'

They still didn't reply. The town's major sports centre, not counting the football stadium, was built around the same time I was born, designed to provide cheap facilities for the locals to enjoy and get fit. It was popular once, but when austerity and cuts to the council kicked in, neither the resources nor the people were left to save it.

When we pulled up outside, the place was lit up like a Christmas tree. If Thompson wanted to keep this event on the QT, this wasn't the way to do it. Dozens of cars were already there, along with a queue of people. Chuck's mate drove us around to the back and parked near an exit. I slipped out of the car and waited for instructions.

Chuck pointed at the door. 'In there, Walker.'

I pushed inside and straight into a set of changing rooms. I recognised some faces from Lydia's photos as silence fell upon the room like a disease, with every eye turned to me. I ignored them all, searching for the Russian and the guy with the Popeye arms, but they weren't there.

Chuck put his hand on my back and pushed me forward. It was another struggle not to lamp him. We walked through a corridor and past a large area with a ring set up in the middle and seats for spectators.

'Your blood will be all over that canvas tonight.'

He appeared to be enjoying himself. At least someone was.

We went through an archway into an office where Thompson was sitting behind a desk. Lydia was by his side, cane in hand and the fat cat at her feet. Three of his goons were dotted around the room. One of them dropped a sports bag near me.

'Your shorts are in there, Frank. I guessed your size, so I hope they fit.' Thompson was also enjoying himself, but Lydia didn't look happy. The moggy was grumpy too. Tony tapped at his expensive watch. 'Get changed. You're in the second bout, so you've got twenty-five minutes to get ready.'

I picked up the bag. 'That's okay. I'll watch the first fight.'

Tony shook his head. 'That's not allowed, Frank. No fighter can observe the others and see how they move.' His grin annoyed me. 'It'll be a big surprise for you.'

'Can you at least tell me who I'm fighting?'

'Of course; his name is Dave Steele.' He pointed a chubby finger at me. 'My money's riding on you, Butcher.'

Everyone laughed, all except Lydia and me. I wasn't sure about the cat. I turned around and headed to the changing area. Chuck and two of the goons followed. As I entered the room, there was loud cheering, and I guessed the first contestants were climbing into the ring.

Three of the others were there with me. I picked an empty corner to get changed. My back was to them, but I knew everyone was calculating how long I could last tonight.

And so was I.

I opened the bag, pulled out the shorts, undressed, and put them on. They were the correct size. Thompson had got something right for a change. They were dark blue and had the letters TT printed in red on each side.

I was a sponsored duck, but how lame would I become?

There was a full-length mirror to my side. Only it wasn't large enough to encompass the whole of my six-foot five-inch frame. It had been a while since I'd admired my reflection, squeezing my arms like an obsessed bodybuilder.

There was a sharp intake of breath when I turned and stuck out my fifty-inch chest. There was fear and admiration in their eyes, and I felt good about that. Maybe they'd thought it was fat and years of unhealthy living under my clothes, but now they could see what kind of physical specimen I was. There was a bit of bulk around my waist, but it wasn't something I couldn't remove if I started exercising regularly. It was another promise I made to myself for new beginnings on Monday.

Someone opened the door and a roar followed them inside. I noticed the cat before I saw her.

'They put the two weakest in first to get the crowd going. The wardens don't want any easy fights: the longer it's drawn out, the more money they'll make on the changing odds.' She held the cane behind her neck as if auditioning for a role in a steampunk movie. She scrutinised every inch of my half-naked torso, and a sudden unexpected heat overtook my face. 'If the punters could see through my eyes now, your odds would be the shortest of the lot.'

'Where did I start on the list?'

'Some people had you as long as twenty to one. Of course, Uncle Tony dumped a load of cash on that.'

'Was that to win my first bout or the whole thing?'

'That was for you to be champion. If I didn't hate gambling, I'd have backed you at those odds myself.'

Wild cheering slipped under the door.

'Your faith in me is touching.'

'That's because she doesn't have a clue about anything.'

Chuck appeared to be braver than usual. 'It's your time for a beating, Walker.'

The cat peered at me through curious eyes as I followed Chuck out. I could have crushed his head there and then, but for the two other goons with him. The noise from the crowd increased the closer we got to them. As we entered the arena, the smell of blood, sweat, and tears assaulted my senses. Somebody dragged a bruised individual from the ring as the multitude chanted a name.

'Stryker, Stryker, Stryker.'

There was no sign of the loser, but plenty of blood on the canvas. Stryker wobbled towards the changing room. Perhaps it was wrong of me, but I hoped he'd be my next opponent.

'Get in, Walker.'

Chuck pointed to the ring, his finger so close to my face I could have leant over and bitten it off.

The canvas was damp with sweat and other stuff I didn't want to think about. The excitement in the crowd had simmered to a low hum until they saw me. Then it transformed into a deathly hush as I stood in the middle of the ring, my gaze travelling around the hall. There must have been a thousand people there.

Silence engulfed every corner for an eternity until their voices exploded into a sonic rush. I was there on my own, with no sign of my opponent yet, so I couldn't tell if they were shouting for or against me.

Then he climbed into the ring on the other side, smaller, leaner, and younger than me. If you'd stood us side by side and tried to guess who would win, few would go for him. But that meant nothing; over the years, I'd seen plenty of smaller fighters take out their bigger and brawnier adversaries. Overconfidence could be my worst enemy.

Noise exploded from hidden speakers, some god-awful tune by Robbie Williams. If this guy hurt me as much as the music did, I'd be in trouble. He gazed at me, a face full of red eyes and a thousand-yard stare.

A third person got in with us, a man in a suit who I assumed was there to address the heaving crowd. And he didn't disappoint.

'Get ready for our next fight, people.' There were no ladies and gentlemen or boys and girls in the audience. He raised his arms into the air and strode around the ring. Then he pointed at me. 'Here's Butcher.'

Then at my opponent.

'Versus Steele.'

The roar took the roof off, loud enough to distract me. The announcer slipped out of the ring as Steele punched me in the side of the head. I staggered to my left and into the ropes. The noise was bloodcurdling this time. I'd only been there for a few seconds, and I'd already made a mistake.

He was on me before I could right myself. I tried to raise my arm for protection, but he buried his face in my flesh, biting through my skin, his saliva like battery acid in my veins.

I howled as I threw him across the canvas, my blood following him through the air. He'd bitten deep and I needed something to stop the flow. The longer I bled, the weaker I'd get.

He crouched on the other side, grinning like Gollum, and my defeat was what he was searching for. He stared at me, not attacking again when I expected him to. I assumed he was waiting for me to make a mistake because I was dazed and confused. Or maybe he knew I couldn't survive another fourteen minutes of this. He wouldn't be wrong.

The blood kept on coming even though I pressed my hand over the wound. How could I have been so stupid? And slow. If I moved at him, he'd sidestep me with ease. I took two steps towards him to prove the point, and he slid to his left. The canvas was spotted red at my feet.

As I glanced down at the stains, Lydia stared at me from the front of the crowd. The disappointment in her eyes was damning. She pointed at my arm.

'We can have that stitched up if you win this fight, but you'll need to do it quickly.'

Well, thanks for that, Lydia.

But how was I going to do that in this state?

I wanted to sit down. Even if I won the fight, I'd be in no fit state for the others if I didn't get this wound stitched up. So I did the only thing I could think of.

I removed my sponsored shorts and wrapped them around the bite on my arm. The material was thick, and though only using one hand hampered me, the blood stopped.

The crowd fell into a shocked silence as they watched me patch up my arm, gazing at me in my birthday suit in the ring. I couldn't worry about standing there in my nakedness or what anyone thought of my middle-aged physique.

Steele must have realised his gambit of waiting me out wouldn't work now. He flew at me. Springing from the corner with his fist raised, he brought it down towards my face, but I dodged it. I could have swung my other arm around and into his head, but I didn't want to dislodge my makeshift bandage.

He was resting on the ropes, watching as my damaged arm flopped at my side. I only had one good arm, and he knew it. If I lunged at him, he'd duck away with his extra speed. I needed him to attack me again, so I could grab him.

But how would I get him to?

He looked in no hurry, so I sat on the canvas. The crowd booed. Then they shouted his name.

'Steele, Steele, Steele.'

I glanced at him while peering at the mass. The tension in the hall increased to boiling point as they shouted for him.

'Steele, Steele, Steele.'

How could he ignore such devotion? So I took a risk, turning my back on him and to them. It was a calculated danger, but I needed to draw him in.

That's when I saw the red-haired man in the mob. He wore a baseball cap and dark glasses, but it was impossible not to see the long, curly red hair falling over his shoulders. He grinned, raising a gloved hand and waving a finger at me.

My gaze was fixed on him when I heard Steele make his move. I expected it this time, jumping from the canvas to meet him head-on. My face smashed into his stomach, squashing my nose. Pain shot through my cheeks, but it didn't matter, my velocity sending us both into the ropes. My heavier physique pinned him there, so I brought my good arm around and grabbed his throat.

I squeezed hard. As I did, the red-haired man moved forward, smirking at me. There was no doubt in my mind this was Harpo. Whether Rose had released the homeless bloke or this was someone else didn't matter. I had to finish this fight and get him.

I dropped Steele to the floor, his fingers grasping at his throat. The crowd went wild. Harpo disappeared into them as I staggered towards him.

A hand was on my shoulder as I tried to climb out. Steele had discovered some reserves of strength and pulled me back. He gave me a one-two punch in the guts, but something rooted my legs into the canvas. I brought up my good arm and punched him in the face with all the muscle I had.

His nose splattered with blood and bone flying everywhere. He collapsed as pain shot through my hand. I tried to ignore the agony as I scrutinised the crowd, twisting my head to find Harpo again.

But he was gone, vanished inside a swarm of furious punters.

Before I knew what was happening, the announcer held up my good arm.

'And the winner is Butcher!'

The buzzing in my skull drowned out the noise from the people.

Someone else was in the ring and guiding me out. I wiped the sweat from my eyes, amazed to see Lydia helping me.

'Well, that was a complete mess; you used nothing I showed you.'

She led me down the steps.

'You didn't teach me to avoid being bitten.'

'I thought that was a given, Walker. I didn't teach you how to suck eggs, but I assume you know how to.'

Her fingers were in mine as we left the hall, taking me to the changing rooms. I needed a lie-down and a couple of shots of whisky.

'Just admit it, Lydia; you're a terrible teacher.'

A sense of euphoria competed with unbearable agony and sped through every inch of me. The tiles were cold against my feet. I hadn't felt them earlier, but now they cut right through me. Blood dripped from my wound and down my naked body.

'We've got thirty minutes to get you into fighting shape.'

'Good luck with that.'

'A doctor is waiting to stitch you up; we might get some painkillers from her.'

It sounded good to me. Even with the differences in height and weight, she dragged me to a bench. Then a woman arrived, removed the bloodied shorts from my arm, and took a needle and thread to my wound after she'd cleaned it.

'Get him more shorts; we can't have him fighting naked again. This is a respectable family show we have here.'

I glanced up at the owner of the voice. 'You always were one to protect your investments, Tony.'

He placed a hand on his chest. 'You pierce my broken heart, old friend. I'd tell the good doctor here to pump you full of painkillers, but I'm afraid that's against the rules. That's why these gentlemen are here to watch over you.'

He moved to the side so I could see the others in the room, black-suited blokes I hadn't noticed before.

'You're too kind.'

The doctor finished up as Thompson stepped away. He'd always hated the smell of blood. She put a bandage on my arm. I assumed it wouldn't last long in the ring. Some goon handed me new shorts. I placed them over my groin and left them there.

'That was some entertainment from you, Frank. After ten years, I don't think any of us have seen anything like that before.'

'He was here, Tony; did you see him?'

'Who was here?'

'You know who. It was Harpo, the man who killed

George Cook, who attacked Grace Marsh, who set me up, and who abducted Dolores.'

I didn't look to him for a response, but fixed on Lydia; just how much did she know about her uncle's operation? She was steely-eyed, but I noticed a tremble in her fingers as she gripped the cane.

'You're delirious and delusional, Frank, a bit like your old man. Get some rest and be ready to earn me more money. I've got another large bet riding on your next bout.'

He left as I wished all my pain away.

'Who is this redheaded bloke?'

Did I detect concern in Lydia's voice?

I tried to move my damaged knuckles, but the discomfort was too much.

'His name's Harpo. He's a killer who's got it in for me.'

She sat opposite me, the cane pressed between her hands. I expected the cat to leap at me from behind her shoulders, but it didn't.

'Why is he out to get you?'

'I don't know, Lydia. The police thought they'd caught him, but I saw him in the crowd during the fight.'

A curious look overtook her face. 'Are you sure you saw him? You were in a lot of pain up there, and that can play tricks on the mind. I know this from experience.'

Was she talking about the loss of her mother or something else?

'I'm still in a lot of pain, but I know what I saw. When I moved towards him, he disappeared into the crowd. Can you look for him while I'm in the ring?'

I'm not sure why I asked her to do this, but she didn't refuse.

'Why would I do this for you?'

I leant against the wall. 'If you want the best for your

community, for this town, as you told me, then leaving a killer on the loose wouldn't be a good thing, would it?'

She stood. 'Get some rest, Walker. You'll be back in the ring soon.'

Then she left me there, alone with those goons.

I wasn't there long. Ten minutes later and Chuck banged on the wall.

'It's time for more punishment, Butcher.'

If you could have stitched together the Cheshire Cat's face with the Joker's maniacal grin, then he was wearing it. I stood and put the shorts on, my wounded arm throbbing as if it was inside a car exhaust.

'Do you still wish you were in the fight, Chuckie?'

His laugh was as crazed as his eyes. 'I wouldn't have made the schoolboy mistakes you did, Walker.' He shook his head. 'Popeye Arms will finish you now, and Mr Thompson will be pissed off. That's when me and the boys get to have some fun with what's left of you.'

I followed him out, promising myself that no matter what happened tonight, I'd make him suffer.

The crowd appeared to have grown as we got outside, even though I'd have sworn there was no room to fit any more people in there. The noise was just as boisterous as before, but there were no shouts of my name. Some of my ego had enjoyed the admiration, but I couldn't let it distract me.

When I climbed into the ring, Popeye Arms was already there. He was a good six inches smaller than me, with a weaker looking chest; the only impressive thing about him were those freakish arms. It looked as if some mad doctor had blown up a few balloons and then sewn them inside his skin.

Lydia had taught me to be evasive, to avoid being hit,

and then strike back with my palm or the bottom of my foot. That was supposed to prevent me from getting too many injuries that would disadvantage me in the final, if I got there.

Now, I had a bandaged arm and bruised knuckles. Trying to block those balloon arms would end up with me on the canvas and him leering at me. I could move my damaged arm, use it to get a blow in, but apart from the pain, there was also the possibility it could open up the stitches in my wound, and then I'd be bleeding again. It was possible to punch with my bruised hand, but not recommended. Whatever I'd need to do to win this fight would hurt my last bout.

If I got there.

All of this went through my head as the announcer called our names and stepped out of the ring. As soon as he slipped through the ropes, I knew there was only one thing I could do.

I moved forward and kicked Popeye Arms in the balls. He crumbled like a wedding cake thrown against the wall. There was stunned silence in the hall. I waited for the crowd to call my name. But all that came was the booing and the hissing.

I stepped back and admired the results of my footwork. Popeye Arms wasn't getting up.

Now there was only one fight left to get my family out of Thompson's corrupt grip.

29 BUTCHER BABY

They had to roll Popeye Arms out of the ring. The mob continued to boo as I climbed out. Some sensation returned to my sore knuckles and I could squeeze my hand, which was welcome since I expected I'd need it for my last fight.

There was no one to greet me this time as I got down, but the crowd parted any way. There was frenzy and heat around me, snarling faces with alcohol-fuelled eyes. There was no redheaded man, no dark gloves reaching for my throat. I assumed he'd still be there, hiding somewhere among the horde, waiting to pounce on me when I was at my weakest.

Lydia was at the door when I entered the corridor.

'Nice to see you learnt something from me.'

I lifted my bandaged arm and wiped the sweat from my lips.

'You don't spend twenty-five years as a copper if you can't handle yourself on the streets.'

The booing changed to cheers as I turned my head and

saw the last combatants enter the arena, glimpsing the Russian as I left; even from a distance, he appeared untouched from his first bout.

Lydia tapped me on my arm with her cane.

'Don't focus on them; keep your mind clear.'

That was easy for her to say since she wasn't the one likely to end up with him in the ring.

'Did he win his previous fight with no trouble?'

She guided me down the corridor. 'Don't think about him until you're face to face. Let's get inside. You might not have much chance to recuperate.'

That told me she expected this next bout to be short and not so sweet.

'Did you have any luck finding Harpo?'

Lydia stopped me before we entered the changing rooms.

'I'm sorry, Walker; I didn't have the time. Uncle Tony had me running an errand for him.'

I didn't ask her what it was because I didn't want to know. So instead, I pushed through the door, surprised to see nobody waiting for me. I slumped into the same spot on the same bench, unsure which part of me hurt the most. Even with the door closed, the crowd's roar was unmistakable.

'That's okay, Lydia; it's just one more thing for me to do once I finish here.' I put my hand on her shoulder, expecting her to flinch, but she didn't. 'Perhaps after tonight, you can get away from this life. You must realise Tony will end up in prison, and if you hang around for too long, he'll take you with him.'

Annoyance flicked across her face. 'You don't listen, Frank. We may operate outside the law, but we provide a lot of benefits to the people here.'

'You mean like the drugs Tony floods the town with?'

She rolled her eyes at me. 'Spoken like a true old man, ex-copper. Soft drugs like cannabis shouldn't be illegal. If you think it's worse than tobacco or alcohol, you're not as intelligent as I thought you were.'

'But it's not just soft drugs. Your uncle and the others are dealing the hard stuff in neighbouring towns and cities and pocketing a huge profit from other people's misery.'

The shock registered on her face before she could hide it, her eyes growing wide as her lips trembled.

'That's a lie.'

I wouldn't argue with her. It seemed she was unaware of everything Tony was up to, but I had to focus on my next challenger.

'So, how do I beat this Russian?'

My quick change of topic didn't faze her.

'Before tonight, the Russian had a record of twenty wins and no losses.'

'Well, thanks for cheering me up. Do you have any more positive stats for me?'

'We need to be practical here, Walker, and get your tactics sorted out.'

'Have you seen this guy fight?'

There was a massive cheer from outside, which took the roof off. The look in Lydia's eyes told me she thought the bout was already over.

'Yes, but not for long. He can take a punch, then aims for the throat, and it only takes one hit there to knock most people out. So you have to protect yourself and find his weak spot quickly.'

She didn't need to tell me this, but I appreciated the concern.

'Are you doing this for Uncle Tony's sake, or are you worried about me?'

'Why can't it be both?'

I smiled through my pain. It was a piece of happiness that didn't last long as Chuck and two goons came into the room.

'Your uncle needs you outside, Lydia.'

She left without another word, glowering at Chuck.

I grinned at him. 'Is it my turn again?'

'How's that bandage holding up, Walker? It looks like it might come off with a quick tug.'

He lunged towards my arm. I took my bruised hand and grabbed him around the throat. The goons never moved. Agony swept through my fingers and into my wrist, but I gripped his slimy flesh. I stood and threw him across the room. He banged his head on a locker and slumped to the floor. Then his colleagues helped him up.

He clawed at his throat and scowled at me.

'You'll pay for this, Walker.' His voice was brittle and trembling. 'I'm going to skin you alive after the Russian pounds you into the canvas.'

'I look forward to seeing you try, Chuckie.'

I moved past him and out of the changing room. The noise coming from the hall was the Stones doing *Street Fighting Man*. Maybe next, they'd play the theme from that *Rocky* movie where he fought a Russian.

Fists were banging on the window as we passed through the corridor, faces squashed against the glass, all distorted as they screamed at me. I couldn't tell if they were for or against me. The goons took the lead into the hall, forcing their way through a mob that wouldn't move. People were pushed to the floor and I stepped over them. This was turning ugly enough to cause problems. But it didn't seem to bother Chuck, who grabbed my good arm and dragged me to the edge of the ring. I shook him off and climbed on to the canvas. He leant into me as I did so.

'You don't know what's going on here, do you, Walker? You don't realise how important I am.'

If I hadn't intended to save myself for the fight, I would have throttled him again.

'Chuckie, you're so forgettable, not even your reflection would recognise you.'

'This isn't the main event, Butcher Boy; you're just the warm-up.'

The noise and the crowd were synchronised as the din grew by the second. I moved closer to his irritating smirk.

'What are you on about?'

'When this is over and you're in a bloody pulp in a cell next door, a select few of these people will watch a bunch of teenagers beat the shit out of each other until one of them dies.' He moved from me. 'And neither you nor anyone else can do anything about it. Nobody cares about them, Walker; nobody important, at least.'

My head was spinning as he slipped away. I turned to the side and the announcer was already in the ring. He spoke to the crowd, but I couldn't make out his words as my arm ached and my fingers throbbed. The canvas shook underneath my toes. I looked from the screaming mob and towards the man who'd entered the ring as the announcer had left: here was the Russian. He pointed at me and the horde went wild.

He spoke, but I didn't hear what she said. This was more than the noise in the hall; there appeared to be something wrong with my ears. The Russian slapped his hands together and bounced up and down. The movement vibrated through the canvas and added to the ringing in my head.

The Russian strode towards me. He threw a fist at my face and I held both my arms up. His knuckles glanced off my flesh and I moved to the side. My balance was off, legs trembling as I stumbled into the ropes. I was weak and sore, and my hand throbbed.

The crowd goaded us on, though I doubt my adversary needed more encouragement. He was quicker than I expected, reaching down and grabbing my shoulder. He dug his fingers into my muscle and hauled me up. I was a rag doll in his grip as he raised his other hand. I found whatever strength I had left in my legs and pushed. My head hit his gut and forced him back. He let go as we tumbled down together like drunken windmills.

I rolled away from him, but he was on his feet before me. As I tried to get up, he kicked me in the ribs. A volcano exploded inside me, but I fought through it. My bandaged arm swung around, my hand grabbing his foot. I twisted it in the opposite direction, the snap of his ankle clearing the hum in my ears.

He squirmed and hit me with his other leg. I rolled him over and got up as the crowd cheered me on.

'Butcher, Butcher, Butcher.'

I wanted to turn from him and look for Harpo, to see how Lydia was reacting to what I'd told her. But I focused on my opponent.

We were both hurting, yet I felt sure he was worse than me. The Russian crawled into the corner. Behind him, in the shadows outside the ring, was Chuck. Thompson's right-hand goon whispered to the Russian, and then slipped something into his hand. I think I was the only one who saw it.

He used the ropes to lift up. There was a glint between his fingers, the reflection from a small blade. Did Chuck hate me that much he'd break the rules in front of all these people? Or was this some plan of his to take over Thompson's empire? Was he lying about forcing kids to fight for their lives?

The Russian lunged at me. It looked like he was throwing a punch at my face, but I saw the dagger. I thrust my bandaged arm up and caught his fist in my fingers. My hand was bigger than his and I crushed it into the knife. His scream was beyond language, but not beyond pain. Blood burst from his fist as he dropped the weapon to the canvas.

Then I punched him in the throat. He fell back and collapsed. I moved over and put my foot on the blade. Did any of the crowd see it? What did I care anyway?

Chuck was in the ring before I knew it. He held up my arm and leant into my face.

'If you know what's good for you, you'll keep quiet.'

'Does Tony know what you're up to?'

There were boos from the mob, but most were chanting my name.

'Butcher, Butcher, Butcher.'

He ignored my question and pushed me towards the crowd. As they rushed forwards, he bent down and grabbed the blade. I climbed out of the ring before he could plunge it into my spine.

Confusion reigned inside my skull as happy punters grasped at me and continued to shout my name. Chuck and the goons removed me from my new fans and shuffled me out of the hall and into the changing rooms.

Once we were through the door, he pushed me into the

corner. Every inch of me ached as I turned to him. His cronies flanked him and there was no way I could take on the three of them in my condition.

'If you're going to kill me, you'd better get on with it.'

Chuck stuck the blade into the bench and laughed at me.

'You're so clueless, Walker.'

Perhaps I could reach for the knife before he did. As I considered this idea, Tony and Lydia entered. He appeared as happy as Larry, while she looked as if someone had killed that annoying cat of hers. Tony gave me a wide grin.

'You've lost me a lot of money, Frank, but I know how you and your old man can make up for that.'

'You bet against me?'

'Once we fixed up your reputation and you performed better in your first two fights than we'd expected, your odds were shorter than the Russian's, but I felt sure he'd beat you.' He sat next to Chuck's blade. 'Still, with one hand, you lose, but with another, you win. Now you'll get your dad to buy his house and hand it over to me.'

'There were no gambling debts, were there? It was all a bluff, a lie you told him in his confused state, and you even had those fake betting slips you were willing to give me.'

'I knew you wouldn't take them. An overbearing sense of morality has always possessed you.' He turned to his niece. 'You should leave now, Lydia. Things are about to get somewhat violent.'

'Is it true what Chuck bragged about, that you're organising fights between teenagers and forcing them to beat the crap out of each other? Is that where some of the missing refugee kids have gone?'

He ignored me. 'It's time to leave, Lydia.'

'Did you tell her about the drug dealing you do outside the town? What else have you kept from her?'

Before I knew it, he'd snatched up the blade and had it at my throat. Chuck and the goons dragged Lydia out as Tony pressed the dagger closer to my flesh.

Was this the way I'd die?

30 LEAN ON ME

They frogmarched me to the sports hall. It was empty of people, but stank of blood, sweat, and tears. I wondered how much of those I had left to give. It didn't take long to find out.

Two goons on each arm heaved me to the ring, pushing me back between the ropes, my arms spread-eagled on the canvas, my neck craning up. Thompson strode towards me, twirling the dagger in his hands. This dexterity with the fingers must have been a Thompson family trait.

I was searching for Lydia when Tony plunged the blade into the hand of my bandaged arm. I don't know if I'd screamed before in my life, maybe as a baby when I was supposedly dropped on my head in the hospital, but I did then – a loud, gurgling shriek that disturbed the dust from the rafters.

The goons held my arms as I tried to tear myself free. Thompson pushed harder until I was pinned by one hand to the canvas. Only then did he let go and stand back, admiring his handiwork with that same satisfied grin that had always wound me up when we were kids.

'Does losing money make you this mad, Toenail?'

The words crawled between my lips, fighting their way out of the fire surging through me.

His mouth parted a centimetre, projecting a cruel, vicious smirk. If he'd sharpened his teeth, he could have been mistaken for a vampire.

'How did you get to be a detective when you're this slow on the uptake?'

I had to keep talking to distract myself from the pain.

'Why don't you enlighten me, then?'

'This wasn't about money, Frank. I didn't bet against you. I know you too well for that. No, once I got over the shock of your return, this was all about paying you back. Of course, if I made a bit of cash along the way, it was fine, but it was never my priority.'

The blood slipped between the edge of the blade and my skin to drip on to the canvas.

'Pay me back for what? You're making less sense than usual.'

He stepped towards me and I expected him to produce another knife for my other palm. He wanted to crucify me, and it was only a question of how long I'd have to wait for it. There was a curious look in his eyes, as if he was an explorer discovering a new species for the first time and he couldn't quite work out what it was.

'After everything you did to me and others, including your brother, I was glad you left, but I didn't realise what effect it would have on Ruby.'

'Your sister? I barely knew her.'

'Yes, but she was head over heels in love with you.'

'She was just a kid.'

I had no memory of what she looked like or even the sound of her voice.

'Indeed, she was, six years younger than us, an impressionable fourteen-year-old when you ran away to the big city. I'm not sure how long she'd had this unrequited love for you. She never spoke about it, but it must have been for a while. Most people get over such a thing, but she didn't. I was twenty-five when it happened to me. It was one of my bosses where I worked, and it was euphoric and soul-destroying at the same time. You go through points where you think life has the greatest potential, only to sink into the darkest and deepest of pits.'

'You're not making any sense, Thompson.'

His tone was sombre and full of regrets.

'Most people survive such heartache, but I can't imagine how bad my sister took it at that age. It wasn't long before she went into a downward spiral with drink and drugs, plus numerous older men she should never have been involved with.' It was anger in his voice now. 'And that's how she met Lydia's father.' He spat the word to the floor. 'He was a heroin addict who dragged her down with him, but I pulled her out of it. It took a long time to get her back on track, but then, of course, nature intervened most horribly.'

If there hadn't been blood seeping from my hand, I might have felt sorry for him. I had sympathy for Lydia, wondering how much she knew of her mother's tragic life.

But I wasn't responsible for what had happened to her.

'You can't blame me for any of that.'

He leant over me, the smell of his aftershave invading my wobbling senses.

'I do, though, Frank. And you've got plenty of other things to answer for, not least the scars you left me with.'

There was madness inside his eyes. 'I never touched you, Tony.'

'Not with your fists.' He grabbed my mouth, squeezing

my lips together until I thought they'd become one. Then he let go. 'You didn't need to hit me or the others because we were so far beneath you. It was the constant ridicule, the put-downs and the demeaning words that wore me down. You were above me and everybody else. Even so, you had to keep pushing, with the name-calling to belittle everyone around you, burying our bodies under your insults to make you feel better. I don't know what happened to you in that house, Frank, but it must have been bad for you to take it out on the rest of us like that.'

'You're talking nonsense, Tony.'

Was he? A whole flurry of repressed memories had poured out of him. Was I really responsible for all of this?

'You don't realise what that does to people, what it does to kids.' He turned his hands into fists. 'I had to put up with it. Put up with you for ten years.' He stood over me with fire in his eyes, his face all puffed up like a balloon ready to explode.

Then the anger evaporated and he laughed.

'Well, after all this time, that was a release.'

'So, this was all to get back at me: taking the house from my father; getting the Cooks to frame me; and paying the red-haired loon to attack people – all because of things which happened when we were kids?'

Thompson pushed the sweat from his eyes. 'None of that was to do with me. I didn't know what you were on about when you spoke about your old man buying his house. I played along with it to wind you up. It was the same with the phantom gambling debts.' He laughed at me. 'As if I'd let anyone owe me that much, never mind a bloke about to shake hands with the Grim Reaper.'

'Didn't George Cook owe you money?'

'Maybe a few hundred quid, that's about it. I don't know

who this red-haired man you keep going on about is. And anyway, I thought the pigs had arrested someone for that.'

With the way the goons had me pressed down, it was difficult to see Thompson's face.

Was he lying?

'That was another stitch-up. Harpo was here tonight, in the crowd. You must have had something to do with it.'

He climbed into the ring and peered at me.

'Nope, nothing to do with me, but I'm happy for whoever it is to keep tormenting you.' He crossed his legs and sat next to me. 'Things couldn't have gone better; to see you in so much physical and mental pain is exquisite.'

'I'm happy for you.'

No matter how I struggled, it was impossible to break away from my captors. Finally, he placed his hand on the dagger and twisted it into my flesh.

'But what do we do with you next?' He looked at his thugs. 'What do you reckon, Chuck?'

I couldn't see Chuck, but I heard his nasal whine.

'He knows about the kids, so...'

Thompson let go of the blade and peered into my eyes.

'As an ex-copper, you must know there's more money in moving people around than drugs or goods. They're much cheaper to acquire, and you can use them more than once. So now we have an influx of children most people don't care about.' He grinned at me. 'Can you imagine being so twisted, you want women and children to drown so they don't come to this shitty country?'

I struggled on the canvas. 'Yes, you're so much better, selling people to line your pockets.'

He shrugged. 'It's quite a lucrative trade, I have to say.'

'You're a twisted bastard, Tony; you always have been.

Your problems have nothing to do with me. You were torturing cats and dogs long before we met at school.'

He removed the dagger from my palm and dangled it over my face.

'Don't all kids do that? At that age, we're curious about mortality and have to test it out.'

The point of the blade touched my eye before he brushed it against my cheek.

'You're a fantastic role model for Lydia, aren't you?'

He ran the edge of the weapon over my stomach.

'You're talking about the drugs and the trafficking?' I don't think he wanted a reply, so I didn't provide one. 'Lydia will come around; she always does.'

Before I could say anything, he reached across me and plunged the dagger into my other palm. I didn't scream, the pain adding to the agony racing through every inch of me. Instead, I swung my free hand at him, but it was so weak, I missed by a country mile.

'Get it over with, you sick bastard.'

He twisted the blade further in. 'You always needed to be a martyr, Frank. Well, this is as close as you're going to get.'

Thompson pushed a bit more before removing the knife and standing over me. I rolled from him, trailing more blood on the canvas. I wanted to stand, but my legs wouldn't move.

I stared through the ropes, straight into Chuck's smirk.

'Do you want us to bury him somewhere, Tony?'

What remained of my strength must have been in my head as my brain tried to work out how I'd survive this night. If Chuck and the other goons took me outside, there might be a chance of getting away from them.

Yeah, maybe they'd get distracted by Santa bringing me an early Christmas present.

Tony came over, bent down, and grabbed me by the arm. He dragged me up as I struggled to fight him off.

'Not yet, Chuck. There's plenty of time to play with him. If we keep most of the blood in the ring, it'll be easier to clean up later. We can't leave any trace of him for the pigs to find.' He pushed me against the ropes. If any part of me wasn't in agony, I didn't know where it was. 'And then I'll sort your old man out, Frank. You two never got on; you always told me that, so I'll be doing you a favour.'

'Do you know how much I admire you, Tony?'

Every word that came out of my mouth increased my pain, but it was worth it for the confusion spreading across his face.

'What?'

He pushed his hands against my shoulders. If I'd had any movement in my arms, I could have strangled him. But all I had were my wits.

'I mean, nobody could have worked harder to make themselves more forgettable than you, Tony. I never thought of you for one second in all the time I was away, but it sounds like you've been obsessing over me like a lost paramour. Are you sure the unrequited love for me was from your sister?'

His face was flame red, his fingers trembling as he dug his nails into my flesh. Spit fell from his mouth as he spoke.

'I'm going to enjoy this, Frank, when I think about how far you've fallen from your self-appointed lofty heights.'

'Tony, every word out of your mouth loses its meaning before it's crawled through your lips. But don't worry; the police will be here soon to put you out of your misery.'

That got him startled enough to let go of me and look around the hall.

If only it hadn't been a lie.

Then the lights came on and I heard DI Rose's wonderful voice.

'Nobody move!'

I don't know who was the most surprised to see DI Rose and a dozen uniformed officers swarm into the building, but I know who was the most pleased. However, I wasn't safe yet as Thompson continued to point his dagger at me.

'You're about to be trimmed, Toenail.'

The rumble of feet into the hall must have disorientated him, his face turning ashen grey as he twisted his head left and right to see who the intruders were. I kept my beady eyes on him, considering he was close enough to lunge at me with that blade.

'None of this matters, Walker, because they've got nothing on me. I'll be out of the cop shop in time for a big fry-up for breakfast. Then I'll deal with you and your old man.'

How easy would it have been to stumble into him, wrestle with that blade, and plunge it into his heart? Yet I didn't – because Lydia distracted me as she climbed into the ring. The police were busy rounding up Thompson's goons as she approached him.

'Put the knife down, Uncle Tony.'

He appeared dazed and confused, his eyes glaring wide and gazing into her. Rose's voice was ringing around the room, but I couldn't make out what she was saying. Instead, I focused on the Thompson family drama unfolding in front of me. He waved the dagger in the air, and I wondered if any officers were carrying firearms.

'It was you who did this, Lydia?'

'You kept too many secrets from me, Uncle, terrible secrets which no right-thinking person could harbour and keep their soul.' She pointed her cane towards Rose as the DI approached the ring. 'I've provided them with all the details of your drug production and distribution, including how you hid all the money in the town's local businesses.'

'You broke the security on my computer?' he said.

Lydia laughed. 'Please, Uncle. I've forgotten more about computers than you've had hot dinners.'

'Put the weapon down, Thompson.'

There was no gun in Rose's hand, but Tony dropped the dagger and stared at his niece.

'How could you do this to me, Lydia, after all I've done for you?' He pointed a trembling finger at me. 'How could you do this after what he did to your mother?'

She shook her head. 'Walker did nothing to Mum.' Her voice trembled, and I watched the tears come. 'She did it all to herself. Maybe if she'd had a loving family to turn to, it would have been different.'

For once, I looked at him and questioned how much we had in common. Were the things he said about me, the emotional bullying, all true? I didn't recognise his version of events, but that didn't mean they were wrong. If those memories came back, would I welcome them?

Perhaps I had to wait forty or fifty years, and then they'd all come tumbling out like the old man's were doing now. But who would be there to look after me? I peered at my wounds as the agony slithered through me. Had I used those hands as a teenager to inflict pain on the other kids around me? Or was it my words that had done all the damage? Had I been a bully all this time?

I stared at Thompson, seeing the wounds in his eyes that must have sunk deep into his mind; seeing a man so damaged he couldn't wait to get revenge on me. I was the Butcher to him then as I was now.

But his memories were tainted, corrupted by a perception that was warped thirty years ago and had only got worse. I felt no guilt for his fate or for what I had and hadn't done as a teenager.

Rose put the cuffs on Thompson and read him his rights. I slid down the ropes and slumped into the canvas. Just before the lights dimmed, the last thing I saw was Lydia leaning over me.

I AWOKE SOMETIME LATER, still in my second choice boxing shorts and lying on a hospital bed. Somebody had patched up my wounds, but every part of me felt as if a Poundshop Dr Frankenstein had taken me apart, and then put me back together. I had to sit up before I noticed Lydia in the corner.

'I placed your trophy on the bedside table.'

A small *Subbuteo* model of a footballer holding up the World Cup was on my right. He was wearing a German national shirt.

'Cheers,' I said.

'How are your hands?'

I turned my palms up and peered at them. The medical staff had done a grand job stitching the wounds together, and even though my knuckles were still red-raw, the soreness had disappeared. The scars on my skin resembled a strange northern version of stigmata.

'They're better than my head.' It continued to throb as if a thousand tiny hooligans were getting drunk inside my skull. I glanced at the new bandage on my arm. 'I feel half-naked.'

'That's why I brought you a present.'

She threw a bag on the bed. I opened it to find my clothes.

'The doctors said you can go home, Walker.' Rose was in the room before I realised it. 'I've organised a car to take you back.'

'How did you know what was going on in the sports hall?'

Rose nodded at Lydia. 'She called me on your phone.'

Lydia pointed at the bag. 'That's in there as well.'

I removed it and my clothes to place them on the bed. I looked at her.

'Why did you tell the police about your uncle?'

'There are things which can't be ignored, Frank, no matter how loyal you feel to your family. So after you told me about the kids, I went to his laptop. I already knew his password and it didn't take long to find the evidence. Then I copied everything to a USB drive.'

'She gave us enough to put Thompson and plenty of others away for a long time,' Rose said. 'Including a few coppers.'

I thought of the charming DS Smith and wondered if she'd be enjoying the wrong side of a police interrogation room, but I didn't mention her to DI Rose. Something else concerned me more. I went into the bathroom to put my clothes on. My arms ached, with my hands feeling as if they were inside a microwave turned up to full. I glanced in the mirror, not recognising the harrowed reflection peering at me. Then I returned to the room.

'Do you know what happened to those missing refugee kids, Sara?'

'Not yet, but we have plenty of data on Thompson's trafficking operation in the computer files Lydia gave us. It won't take long before some of those involved spill their guts.' She showed me the card in her hands. 'I'm in contact with the Refugee Service. We'll find those kids.'

Lydia spoke. 'Start with Chuck Jones; he's the weakest of the lot. You'll get nothing from my uncle.'

I sat on the bed, trying to work out Lydia's mental state.

'What will you do now?'

She shrugged and reached for the cane propped against the wall.

'Me and Fudge will be fine. I have my own money,' she glanced at Rose, 'all legally acquired. Perhaps this is the right time for me to start a new adventure.'

Lydia posed the same question to me. 'What will you do next, Walker?'

I checked my phone – it was six o'clock on Sunday morning.

'I've got a meeting with social services tomorrow to discuss my father's future. I'll decide after that.' She seemed concerned for my health, but I needed to tell DI Rose something else. 'I saw Harpo at the fight.'

Rose puffed out her cheeks. 'Lydia told me you thought you'd seen a redheaded man.'

I flexed my aching fingers. 'I didn't think I saw him – I saw him. What's happening with the homeless bloke?'

She shrugged. 'Nothing. We still don't know who he is. However, I need you to come to the station sooner rather than later to give me a statement about the events in the sports hall. We'll talk about it then.' She turned to Lydia. 'Do you want a lift anywhere?'

'Your officers can drop me off when they take Walker home.' She stared at me. 'Is that okay with you?'

'Of course it is.'

We left together, walking past a crowded Accident and Emergency department, which must have included some fighters from last night's little contest.

'Don't forget to visit me at the station,' Rose said to me as Lydia and I got into the back of a police car.

The driver turned to us. 'Where do you want dropping off?'

I gave him my old man's address while Lydia told him to go to the train station.

'You're leaving town?'

I couldn't blame her if she did. Maybe she'd take the same route I did twenty-five years ago. She handed me a key and a card with an address on it.

'I need you to look after Fudge while I'm away. I'm not sure when I'll return, but I will once I sort my head out.'

It can't have been easy for her. She'd done the right thing, but it was still a betrayal of the uncle who'd looked after her since her mother's death.

'Do you know where you're going?'

'No, but that's what makes it so exciting.'

I nodded. We were silent for the rest of the journey

until we reached the train station and she was ready to get out of the car.

'Was it true what Tony said, about how your mother felt about me?'

Lydia smiled. 'She was a troubled woman. I think everyone in my family has been troubled somehow, but she only had nice things to say about you.'

'She spoke about me?'

'You were the one who got away. Haven't you ever had one of those, Frank?'

I thought of Alisha and the good times we'd had together. I pushed away the bad memories.

'Yeah, kid, I have.'

She stepped out of the car. The first trains were due soon.

'Should I go north or south?'

'Do what I did twenty-five years ago, Lydia: toss a coin.'

The car pulled away as the sun illuminated the journey. The painkillers were kicking in and I could move my hands without too much irritation. The police dropped me off ten minutes later.

The curtains were closed in the living room, but the light was sneaking out from the middle. I wondered if the old man had slept downstairs or just left all the lights on when he'd gone to bed.

I removed the key and opened the front door, then went to the kitchen for a drink of water. I took more painkillers to ease the agony at the back of my head.

When I went into the living room, my father was in his usual seat. The TV was off, but he was awake and staring at me. Only he wasn't looking at me, but at something over my shoulder.

God, what if he'd had a stroke?

I rushed to him.

'Dad, are you okay?'

'He's fine, Frank; no thanks to you.'

The voice was behind me, one I hadn't heard in a very long time.

Then the barrel of a gun was at the nape of my neck.

32 GUN FURY

The metal of the gun chilled my neck. He pushed it further into my skin and forced me on to the sofa. I tumbled into the middle, my damaged hands finding what was there: a baseball cap and a red-haired wig. I grabbed the fake curls and straightened up to turn to him.

'You look like you've been in the wars, Frank.'

A short, stocky bald man pointed a gun at me. His eyes were bloodshot, face sallow and unshaved. He wore thick gloves and was dressed all in black. He wasn't there to give me a box of chocolates. I glanced at my father; his gaze focused on us as I picked up the wig.

'That's a great disguise, Tommy.'

He grinned at me. 'Well, little brother, I had to make sure our reunion was at the right moment.' He waved a gloved hand at the walls and I noticed there was something unusual with the movement of his fingers. 'And it could only take place here.'

'You were at the fighting competition?'

He nodded. 'I had to see you in action. I got a bit too close to the ring, but I saw what I needed to.'

I threw the wig to the floor. 'It was you who killed George Cook, who attacked Grace Marsh. Why?'

He kept the weapon pointed at my head. 'It's a long story, Frank, but it's all your fault.'

It appeared I was to blame for everything wrong in this town.

'Why?'

I had to keep him talking until I could figure a way of taking the gun from him without getting shot or a ricochet hitting the old man.

'You know, Frank. You ran away to pretend the past never happened, but being here is bringing it all back. You're remembering what you did to me, aren't you?'

He held up his gloved hand, the one which was gun-free. Something about it wasn't right, but I couldn't tell what it was. My brother kept the weapon trained on me and raised his other hand to his mouth. He used his teeth to remove the glove and discarded it on to the floor.

Then I saw what was wrong.

Three fingers were missing from above the knuckles. This was why he couldn't put full pressure around the throats of his victims. I peered at the absent digits as the memory returned to me.

It was thirty-five years ago inside this house. I was playing with the sharpest of the kitchen knives, practising some trick I'd seen in a movie. I plunged the blade in the gaps between my fingers with my hand placed on the table. I'd started slowly, but then picked up speed, missing my flesh every time, but only just. It was an adrenalin thrill, a sense of euphoria I haven't experienced since.

The memory was in my head, but I could see it in his eyes, like ghosts haunting us both.

'You remember, don't you, Frank, getting me to place

my hand on the table so you could weave your magic with the kitchen knife?'

The image came crashing back to me.

'I was a kid, Tommy; you were the grown-up. I could never make you do anything you didn't want to.'

He shook his head. 'The ten years between us made no difference; you know that. You were always the more mature one. You had the physique and the emotional intelligence I didn't have.'

I couldn't see him now, didn't see the gun, my vision in the past. We were in the kitchen again as I brought the knife down, twisting it in my hand so the edge of the blade sliced through his fingers. The blood was everywhere, his screams returning me to the present.

'It was an accident, Tommy.'

That's what I'd always told myself. But why did I twist the knife, so it cut through three of his fingers?

'No, Frank, you did it on purpose. Do you remember why?'

I shook my head. 'It was an accident, Tommy.'

The two remaining fingers on his damaged hand trembled. I stared at the wounds in my palms as he spoke.

'You were jealous of the one thing I could do better than you. So you made sure I wouldn't play the guitar again.'

The sound of music sprang into my mind, slipping out from the speakers hidden inside the shadows of my brain.

'We were in a band.'

'Yes.' He waved the gun at me. 'Me and my mates needed another guitarist, and you'd been playing since you were eight; we were desperate, so we took you.' I stared at my hands again. I had played the guitar so long ago. 'But you couldn't handle it, could you? So that's why you did this.'

He lifted his damaged hand into the air.

That was the day I ran out of the house and into the road; the day the bus nearly hit me; the day Bullock swerved her car to miss me.

'You joined the army soon after.'

His grin looked painful. 'Can you believe they took me like this?' He waved those two lonely fingers again. 'I guess they must have been desperate.'

'But you ran away from them, you disappeared.'

'I stuck it for a year.' His eyes were full of anguish. 'You can't believe how much bullying and intimidation go on in the military. People killed themselves, and they covered up the deaths. Finally, I couldn't take it anymore, so I went absent without leave.'

'Didn't they look for you?'

'They came to this house.' The old man's voice shook me. It was fragile and vulnerable.

Tommy stared at him. 'I didn't know that.'

This was my chance to grab the gun and wrestle him to the floor. But I didn't.

'Two of them, military police, turned up one afternoon. It was easy to tell them I didn't know where you were because it was true.'

Sadness seeped out of him.

'What did you do, Tommy?'

'After thirty days of AWOL, it gets classed as desertion. So I was on the run from them for a year before returning voluntarily. I was released with a Dishonourable Discharge.' His glare pierced right through me. 'I've spent thirty years doing shitty jobs and living in the crappiest places, so I decided it couldn't get any worse by returning here.'

He didn't hide the distaste in his mouth. I wondered if

the old man had realised how both his sons had only returned to him because they had no other choice.

'Why did you kill Cook and attack Grace? Was it just to get back at me?'

'I was on my way here when I bumped into George Cook in the pub. Imagine the luck of that, of me sitting next to my new neighbour and him not knowing who I was. Then he went on about how the bloke living next door to him had asked for advice on buying his house for a pittance under the Right to Buy scheme. He couldn't hide it from me, how he was planning to defraud the old man.' Tommy laughed like a strangled cat. 'He was such a blabbermouth when he was drunk. So I said I'd help him, which is when he introduced me to the barmaid. And then you arrived and ruined everything.'

'It was you who wanted this house?'

The gun trembled in his hand. 'It's my legacy, Frank; the only thing of value I'll ever get from this family.' He glanced at our father. 'I came here twice before you turned up, but I don't think he could remember the visits, which was good for me.'

'You tried to frame me, killed George, and attacked Grace so that you could get this house?'

'Don't sound so shocked, brother. Once the paperwork is done and the old man signs the property over to me, there's a hundred grand's worth of profit to be made. Maybe more if I could have bargained it into Thompson's scheme to sell the whole street to property developers. And I wouldn't have had to kill Cook and silence the barmaid if you hadn't returned.' His head and the gun shook. 'Even now, after all this time apart, you're still ruining things for me.'

'What did you do with Dolores?'

He cackled again. 'Cook's stupid wife? I did nothing to her. I searched for her after I killed the husband, but I couldn't find her anywhere. So I guess she did a runner too.'

I pointed to the fake hair on the floor.

'Why the wig, Tommy?'

He shrugged. 'I hate being bald as much as I hate this.' He thrust his deformed hand at me.

'You planted the gloves on the homeless man?'

He waved the gun at me. 'It was fate, little brother, me stumbling across a down-and-out redhead like that under the bridge.'

'Did you know he was mute?'

He laughed at me. 'Really? No, I didn't know that. I told Grace his name was Harpo as a joke.' His laugh irritated every one of my bruises. 'The killing joke, eh?'

'So, you're going to shoot me. How will you cover that up?'

'I've been thinking about that.' He glanced at the old man. 'You don't want to upset him, do you?'

'I'd prefer not to.'

'Get up then.' He used the gun to direct me towards the door. 'Let's go into the dining room, the place where you did the dirty deed.'

We went down the corridor, through the kitchen, and into the back. I stood next to the bookcase near the far wall.

'This is madness, Tommy; you know that.'

'All human existence is futile and insane, Frank; why is this any different?' If he wanted an answer, I didn't give him one. 'I've been carrying your baggage around with me for most of my life. It's time for me to put it down and start afresh. And what better way to begin than with the keys to my own castle?'

'And what will you do with our father?'

'He lost the plot ages ago; a care home will be the best place for him.'

'And me?'

He scratched at his chin with his two-fingered hand, a strange sight resembling a praying mantis clicking its legs together. How quickly I'd put this other life behind me, with no remembrance of things past – it wasn't just another country; it was in a different universe.

I wished I'd never come back.

'You've always been a conundrum, little brother.' He reached into his pocket with those two fingers and removed four pills. 'There's a bottle of water on the table. Take it and swallow these.'

'What are they?'

'They're ketamine. They'll put you in a relaxed state.'

I knew what the drug could do: a small dosage, and I'd be chilled and happy, or I'd be confused and nauseated. But if those pills of his were a large dose, I might descend into a "k-hole." That would make me feel as if my mind and body had separated, and I wouldn't be able to do anything about it.

'You're not brave enough to strangle me, are you, brother? You'll drug me with those, and then give me something else when I'm helpless. Then, when the police turn up, they'll think it's either an overdose or suicide. Have you already written a note in my name?'

'What choice do I have, Frank? I've killed once, and that barmaid isn't likely to come out of her coma and identify me, so that only leaves you as a loose end. Once they announce your death, I'll return as the grieving older brother, ready to look after his aged and infirm father. I see now it couldn't have worked out better, with your death being the perfect reason for my return to the family home.'

'But I'm not the only loose end, am I, Tommy?'

'You can't distract me, Frank. Take the pills, or I'll shoot you and think of some excuse later.' Then, an idea appeared to spark inside his flickering brain. 'In fact, all I have to do is put this gun in Father's hand, and that's the problem solved.'

'You're still forgetting one thing, forgetting one more person.'

'Who's that?'

That was when Dolores cracked him over the skull with the porcelain figure of Winston Churchill someone had given to my parents as a wedding gift seventy years ago.

I TIED his hands and feet together with rope from the kitchen drawer. Then I called Rose and told her to come over. When I got off the phone, Dolores was sitting in the living room talking to my father. There was a gleam in his face I'd never seen before. It was as if he was a new parent, staring at his children for the first time.

'I said Thomas and Mary were visiting, didn't I, Frank?'

I took hold of his emaciated hand. 'Yes, you did, Dad.'

And he had, several times, only I'd assumed they were more of his delusions.

Dolores handed me a key. It was the spare to the house the old man had left with the neighbours, just like they'd done with him.

'I thought you'd want this back.'

'You've been living in our attic, haven't you?'

'I didn't know where to go once I knew he'd killed George.'

'Did you know he was my older brother?'

'Not at first. When I was hiding upstairs, I heard him

talking to your father in the house. I was too scared to come down when you were here. I wasn't sure what you'd do to me for lying to the police.'

She wiped a tear from her eye, and I held out my hand in forgiveness.

'I'm just glad you came down when you did. And I forgive you for eating the food I bought.'

'I tried to give your father messages for you, but he was so confused, thinking I was your sister.'

She whispered that to me, but I don't think it mattered. He'd closed his eyes, was snoring away as we spoke.

He was still asleep when Rose arrived with her colleagues ten minutes later. She was amused to see Tommy tied up in the kitchen. And she had good news for me.

'Grace Marsh has come out of her coma. The doctors expect her to make a full recovery. With her evidence and what Dolores tells us, your brother will be behind bars for some time. And we got the redheaded stranger the help he needs – he's at the hospital now.'

She seemed happy with that, but I couldn't smile about any of it. Instead, I watched them all leave, Dolores returning next door and the uniforms carrying my brother out of the house. Rose reminded me to go to the station once I'd had some rest.

I returned to the living room once they'd gone. The old man continued to snore. I sank into the sofa. The police had removed the baseball cap and wig as evidence. I reached into my pocket and got the paper Lydia had given me.

I'd lost a brother but, was about to gain a cat.

THANK YOU!

Thank you, dear reader for purchasing this book.

Many thanks to my wonderful wife for all her support and patience.

Extra special thanks to Karina Gallagher for being a dedicated reader of my work.

Where The Bodies Are Buried edited by Alison Jack.

Cover design by James, GoOnWrite.com